UNCLE RONALD

Brian Doyle

UNCLE RONALD

A Groundwood Book

Douglas & McIntyre

Vancouver Toronto Buffalo

Groundwood Books/Douglas & McIntyre
585 Bloor Street West
Toronto, Ontario M6G 1K5

The publisher gratefully acknowledges the assistance of the
Canada Council and the Ontario Arts Council.

Canadian Cataloguing in Publication Data

Doyle, Brian
Uncle Ronald
"A Groundwood book".
ISBN 0-88899-266-1 (bound) ISBN 0-88899-267-X (pbk.)
I. Title.

PS8557.O87U53 1996 jC813'.54 C96-930310-6
PZ7.D773Un 1996

Cover illustration by Ludmilla Temertey
Design by Michael Solomon
Printed and bound in Canada

CONTENTS

To my grandson Aidan Jeffrey Ray
A.K.A. "A.J."

Here

A CURLED-UP DEAD MAPLE LEAF, ONE OF THE last, limps down the cold, clay path like an old, crippled spider.

I remember that so clear.

I was going for two pails of water.

It was late fall.

Late fall, a hundred years ago.

I'm a hundred and twelve years old and I can't remember what I had for lunch today and I can't remember the name of the nurse who looks after me and I can't tell you the name of the place it is where they've got me living and I can never remember the name of the old geezer I play chess with here every day, but I can remember everything, in vivid detail, about November, 1895, when the army came up from Ottawa to attack the people around the little town of Low.

And I remember that dead leaf blowing down the path.

1

He Liked Me Better Than Her

MY FATHER BEAT MY MOTHER WITH HIS BELT. And when I tried to grab him one time, stop him, he beat me with the belt, too. Now he was beating both of us all the time.

When he beat my mother he would beat her with the buckle end of the belt. But when he beat me he would turn the belt around and hold the other end so that he'd be beating me with the end that didn't have the buckle on.

My mother told me that he did that because he liked me better.

"He uses the buckle end on me because he doesn't like me as much as he likes you," my mother used to say.

When my father decided it was time for one of our beatings he would undo his belt buckle and then pull the belt as hard as he could from around his pants through the belt loops. The tail of the belt would make a loud flapping sound as it came around through the loops. Then it would fly out, coiling in the air like a hateful snake, high up over my mother, high up over me.

Sometimes we'd be lucky and his pants would fall down and he'd have to stop beating us to pull them up and we'd get away—run outside and down the alley.

My father worked on the square timber rafts. The

lumber barons tied the huge timber together and floated them down the Ottawa River to Montreal and then
down the St. Lawrence River to Quebec City. The men
would live on the raft and be gone for weeks at a time.

"There's a raft leavin' in a couple of days," my mother would say. "Let's hope he's on it!" Or she'd say,
"Maybe the raft will break up on them and part of it
will float out to sea with him on it, please, God!"

But then one day my mother was shaking and crying and she told me that he was fired off the rafts for
fighting and now he was going to be home more.
That's about when she started her plan for us to run
away.

But then she changed her mind. She decided to give
him another chance. He was going to change.
Everything was going to be different. She said he was
once a very sweet man. I didn't believe her. Even when
he would sing to her in his so-called beautiful voice.
He'd sing a song with her name in it. My mother's
name was Nora.

There was a new steam mill opened up over in Hull
by the Gilmours and he got a new job over there
dumping waste wood, like sawdust and knots and bark
and log-ends, into the huge furnace that burned all day
and all night to boil the water to make the steam to
drive the saws to cut the logs into lumber.

My father would be home more now. Everything
would be different. But it wasn't.

My father worked up on top where the conveyor
belts dumped the waste wood into the red-hot, white-
hot firepit. His job was to make sure everything went
into the flames. Nothing got stuck, nothing escaped.

And neither did we. The beating started again.

And my mother changed her mind again.

"Good training for him," my mother said, "because in the next world he's going to be engaged in a similar kind of position, only this time, he'll be *on* the conveyor belt!"

One night my father came home and went right to sleep with all his clothes on. My mother's plan was to get his belt off while he was still asleep and tie his hands behind his back with it. Then, when he woke up he wouldn't be able to whip it off and start beating us with it.

He was snoring so loud the windows of our little shack were rattling.

We stood beside him for a long while to see how asleep he was.

"If it wasn't a mortal sin," my mother whispered hoarsely, "I'd take up the ax right now, this minute, and chop his cursed throat!"

My mother undid his belt and we started trying to haul it from around his huge belly. As we pulled together, counting one, two, three each time, he started rolling back and forward. You could hear him sloshing while he rolled. The harder we pulled the more he rolled, but the belt was still caught underneath him.

When he fell off the bed and crashed onto the floor, my mother and I ran and hid.

He was quiet for a while. Then the snoring again.

His opening snore was like an explosion.

The cat stood on tiptoes and arched her back and tried to get rid of all her fur.

My father was on his stomach now. Lying on the

buckle. It was not possible to get that belt off him. It was hopeless.

And he'd be up sooner or later. And then we were for it.

We went to bed. I curled up in my mother's arms and we slept for a couple of hours.

I dreamed my mother's eyes burned like hot coals inside their dark rings.

I dreamed we stood beside my sloshing father.

"Get me the ax!" I dreamed she whispered loud.

I dreamt I felt the feel of my father's hot blood squirting across my cheek.

2

Ways Not to Wet the Bed

MY MOTHER WOKE ME UP EARLY. SHE KNEW I hated waking up, knew I was afraid of waking up, knew that the idea of waking up in the morning filled me with shame and with dread.

The reason for this was I was wetting the bed, pissing the bed every night. I couldn't help it. I couldn't do anything about it. I hated to go to sleep at night because I knew I'd wake up soaking wet and smelling bad. And the mattress all soggy. I was so ashamed. And afraid. Afraid that people would find out. Ashamed and afraid because when you are as old as I was then, you shouldn't be pissing in your bed.

I'd sometimes dream that I was standing over the pot and that everything was all right. Then I'd let go and as soon as I'd let go I'd realize that I wasn't standing over the pot at all, I was dreaming I was standing over the pot and actually I was still in bed and then I'd wake up and it would be too late. And I'd feel the warm on my stomach and my legs.

My mother and I tried everything to get me to quit.

Tried not drinking any liquid after four o'clock in the afternoon. But then I couldn't get to sleep because I was so thirsty. By midnight I couldn't stand it any more and I'd get up and drink about a gallon of water and then go to bed and right to sleep. The next morning I'd be swimming.

Or I'd lie right on the edge of the bed, tight against the wall. Pressed up against where the mattress met the wall. Fall asleep like that if you can. Piss down the wall and the side of the mattress. They'd never know. Wallpaper was all stained from the leak in the roof anyway. But that didn't work because most of the time after I'd fall asleep I'd roll back over onto the deep middle of the bed and be back in the same old fix all over again.

"Oh, poor Mickey," my mother would say in the morning. "What are we going to do with you?"

She'd be ripping the sheet off the bed, turning over the mattress which already had stains on the other side from the times before.

"We've tried everything," she'd say. "We'll have to get the doctor over, see what he says about it!" And then she'd sigh.

She was right when she said we tried everything.

My mother was always reading, and in a story she read to me once by Charles Dickens called *A Christmas Carol*, a famous story, the hero, Scrooge, had bad dreams because of some cheese he ate before he went to sleep.

We thought that if I ate a lot of cheese before I went to sleep I'd have nightmares all night which would take my mind off wetting the bed. The cheese gave me nightmares all right but they were nightmares about wetting the bed. So that didn't work.

I tried tying an empty bean can under the bed to the spring with a wire and digging a hole in my mattress and lying on my stomach over the hole. Didn't work. Wound up with my foot stuck in the hole and the bed soaking wet again.

Tried a clothes pin on my "spigot" as my mother called it but it just caused a lot of pain and one night I nearly exploded.

A nice lady in the next shack who my mother said was a witch told me to try tying cloves of garlic around my waist and my thighs but that just made things worse because urine mixed with garlic smells worse than just plain urine.

The stupidest plan was attaching a hose to myself and hanging it out the window.

There were so many thieves in Lowertown that you couldn't even leave your clothes on the line at night or you'd come out in the morning and they'd be gone.

My father had stolen a hose from the mill where he worked. Brought it home, he said, to beat us with it.

I attached the hose to my spigot with string and a strong, nickel-plated tie clip I found outside Roger the Embalmer's shop in the snow one spring on Bank Street. Then I hung the hose out the window.

Anyway, in the middle of the night, a thief going by saw the valuable hose hanging out the window, grabbed it and ran.

I was sore for about a week after.

I wasn't going to school that year. The year 1895. I passed everything the year before but when I started back in September something strange started happening to me.

Every time I sat in my desk and the teacher said good morning, I'd lose my breath and I'd faint. I'd flop down on the desk like a dead fish and they'd have to haul me out and put me in the cloakroom on some coats on the floor and then get somebody to go to my place and get my mother to come and take me home.

This happened so many times that the school told my mother to keep me at home until the doctor figured out what to do with me. When the doctor finally came over to Lowertown and over to our shack, he decided I'd better stay home from school for the rest of the year and rest up as best I could.

That's what he said.

"Keep him home from school. Let him get rested up."

My mother just looked at him. "Doctors!" she said.

Not too long after that I started wetting the bed.

3

Wishing Somebody Else Was Your Father

MY MOTHER WOKE ME UP GENTLE, SOOTHING, saying she had a plan, hurry, quietly, your father's still on the floor, we have a plan. It was a plan she'd had for weeks.

It was now or never.

She pulled up a board from the floor under my bed and took out a box. In the box there was a new pair of denim overalls, with bib. There was a tag on the overalls: "Half price sale—50 cents. O'Reilly's." There was also a set of woolen combination long underwear, with trap door. The tag on this beautiful underwear said: "Half price sale—60 cents. O'Reilly's." And a little sign: "If O'Reilly made them, they fit."

"I wonder how O'Reilly knows what size you take, Mickey," my mother said.

I rubbed the new woolen underwear into my face. It felt so smooth and smelled so new. It was the nicest piece of clothing I'd ever felt.

My mother had a sack packed for me for a trip. There was a pencil and a pad. A cake of soap and a towel. Socks. A shirt, mitts, scarf, a toque. A bottle of Skiel Cod Liver Oil "for plump cheeks."

There was an envelope with seventy-five cents in. There was a copy of the book *Beautiful Joe* by Margaret Marshall Saunders. There was a packet of tea and a small bag of sugar. And a little paper sack of hard candy.

"You're goin' to stay at the farm with me brother for the winter. You're goin' to get out of this. This is no place for a child."

She broke a loaf of bread in half, wrapped it in newspaper, squeezed it gently into the sack.

"I've been stealing money from your father's pants for weeks now, preparing for this moment in our unfortunate existence!" she was saying as she helped me into my new clothes and put her finger to her lips.

No more talking.

My mother sat at the table and scribbled a note. She scribbled it in a planned kind of way—a note that she wanted to look scribbled in a hurry. She actually was very careful about the scribbling. The note said, "CPR depot—7:00 A.M."

She looked at it to see if it looked right and then she pushed it gently off the edge of the table and watched it flutter naturally under the chair.

She looked at me and winked.

My father would find it there. She hoped.

It was a false clue.

I said a silent goodbye to the cat, rubbing his furry head and touching his cold, wet nose to my lips.

We stepped past my father's body on the floor. I leaned down, looked down in the gloom to see if his throat was axed. But I knew it wasn't. I knew it was just a dream. He was rolled over on his back now. Rolled over during the night. He was half under the bed.

The look on his face—his eyes half open, his mouth gaping, the blood heaving and pumping in the veins in his neck, his flapping cheeks, his caked lips—all these filled me with fear.

We slipped quiet out the broken entrance of our shack. While I was pulling the door shut he let out a roar that made my heart stop. The whole building seemed to shake.

But he wasn't awake. He was just choking on an extra big snore.

We picked our way through the mud between the crooked shacks and went up the dark path to the street.

There were quite a few people in the street. It wasn't even 6:00 A.M. but people were already on their way to their jobs in the mills. The electric streetcars were a new thing then, in Ottawa. They made the street look joyful, and the sound of the bell and the crackling of the wires and the warm glow of the lights gave you a happy feeling, a safe feeling.

The sign on the electric streetcar said Chaudiere Falls. We'd go as far as the turn over to Hull, then get off and walk the rest of the way to the CPR depot.

My mother was going to put me on the train to Low, Quebec, to my Uncle Ronald O'Rourke.

"But not until tonight," she explained. "The real train you'll be on leaves Union Depot at 5:30 tonight. We're going to the CPR depot this morning, pretending to take a train there. West or south or east—he'll never figure it out. We could be headed for Toronto or Halifax or New York as far as he'll ever be able to tell!"

Under one of the new electric streetlights on Rideau Street I saw a small crowd gathered around. The crowd was watching six policemen lined up at attention. They weren't Ottawa policemen. Ottawa police didn't wear knee-length boots so shiny that the new electric streetlight reflected off them, glittered off them. And

Ottawa police didn't have spotless blue uniforms with twinkling gold buttons. And Ottawa policemen definitely didn't wear those tall, fancy, strange-looking hats with the feather plumes and chin straps with tassels.

Ottawa police were usually covered with mud from rolling around in the streets all the time trying to arrest people day and night.

The streetcar was delayed because somebody's pig was on the track and wouldn't move and there was a wagon upset up the street and there were Thanksgiving turkeys running all over the place.

The fancy policemen were being checked over by their captain. They were all tall and handsome in their outfits. And they wore revolvers in shiny black-leather holsters on their broad belts.

"They're not from around here," a man who was standing beside my mother and me on the streetcar said in a loud voice. "Nossir," he said. After he thought for a while about what he just said, he said, "Nossir, they be's from someplace else for sure. Not from around these parts. Definitely from away somewhere else..."

My mother was rolling her eyes. "I suppose if they weren't from around here, they pretty well *have* to be from someplace else!" she said, and everybody on the streetcar laughed.

My mother had no patience with people who said obvious things.

The streetcar got moving again.

"Now, in your sack," my mother was saying, "you have yourself a pad and pencil, and you'll write me a letter every Sunday, tell me how you're making out. Here's the postal box number written on the back of the pad where you'll send it. I won't be where we just left or anywhere near where your father is. But I'll have the mail picked up at the main post office every Monday. And I'll expect a letter there from you, me bucko, without fail, each Sunday! You'll pay the stamps out of the seventy-five cents you've got in the envelope..."

"Seventy-five cents is pretty near a dollar. And a dollar's quite a sum for a young lad to be goin' around with," the man beside us said.

My mother turned on him, her eyes flashing.

"Would it be askin' too much, sir, for you to keep your gob shut and your ugly face out of our affairs!"

Everybody on the streetcar laughed again.

My mother had no patience with people who couldn't mind their own business.

We moved down to the back of the car and my mother continued her instructions.

"Now, you have a cake of soap there. Use it every morning when you get up first thing, no matter how cold it is in your room. And take a spoonful of cod liver oil before you go to bed at night. When that bottle runs out, me second cousins once removed, the O'Malley girls, will supply you with another.

"Now, the tea and the sugar is a gift for me cousins the O'Malley girls. The candy, that's a little treat for the O'Malley girls, too. Have a piece of it from time to time yourself and think of your mother..."

My mother looked at her own reflection in the dark back window of the electric streetcar, and I looked at both our reflections, and while the trolley above us threw sparks into the air and made our reflections flash, we cried a little bit together.

A woman got on the streetcar selling ripe plums. My mother got two for one cent. We ate the plums and by chewing and sucking on the plums, forgot our tears.

The streetcar headed over Sappers' Bridge and up Wellington Street.

We were getting to the Parliament Buildings. I loved looking at the Parliament Buildings. They were so strong and solid and beautiful now with the electric light. And they made you feel proud and safe.

While I shaded my eyes against the streetcar window I saw a beautiful man striding very straight and smooth wearing a tall silk hat and carrying a walking stick and gliding under a streetlamp in front of the Parliament Buildings.

He had on a tall white collar and a long black coat and white gloves.

I was looking at him, wondering what it would be like to have a father like him instead of the one I had.

My mother saw me looking and told me that the man was Wilfrid Laurier. He would someday be called *Sir* Wilfrid Laurier and would be Canada's first French Canadian prime minister, but nobody knew that then.

"There's a kind, good man," my mother said with a sigh. "There's a gentleman. I'll wager my soul he doesn't strike his wife and young ones with his belt!"

Mr. Wilfrid Laurier turned through the iron gates and walked toward the Parliament Buildings.

I wanted with all my heart to have someone like him for a father.

Suddenly a fire wagon clanked by. It was pulled by four wild-acting horses. The wagon was jangling its bells like mad and the firemen were hanging on for dear life as the wagon nearly upset while it passed around the streetcar. Waves of mud were sloshing off the wagon wheels and hoses were flying and buckets and tools were bouncing into the air. People pushed to the front and sides of the streetcar to see what there was to see.

In the distance, west on Wellington Street, the sky was a red glow.

Two more reels went by and people on the street were running.

As the streetcar got closer to the Chaudiere Falls where it would turn to take the passengers over to the mills to work, the sky got redder to the west and it was full of flying showers of flame.

The news came back to us at the back of the electric streetcar.

The CPR train depot was on fire.

4

A Fun Fire

THE BONE-DRY CEDAR SHINGLES, RED-HOT, were flying up and away from the roof of the CPR depot like shooting stars and raining trails of beautiful red and yellow sparks over the Chaudiere Falls. Sheets of red and blue flame were splashing up the tall wood walls of the depot.

Windows were exploding. The crowd was going *ooh!* and *aah!* A lot of people were going to be late for work at the mills over the river that day.

It was hopeless to try and save the building. The firemen were hosing the other sheds around to keep them from going up in flames.

And people further away were gathering pails of water around their little houses and shacks, just in case.

Travelers were trying to save suitcases, boxes, packages. Two men and a bunch of kids were rolling a smoldering wagon full of baggage into a big puddle of mud along the tracks. A man was running with a suitcase on fire, kicking it, hitting it on the ground, dragging it through puddles trying to put it out.

Steam engines were groaning and roaring, banging and shunting boxcars further down the tracks away from the depot, away from the flames.

The platform was now on fire. Yellow tongues licked the planks. Down the way an open coal car had taken too many burning shingles. The coal in the car had ignited. The firemen trained their hoses on the coal. Blue flames and steam exploded into the sky and the crowd cheered.

The water pressure from the new city hydrants was as powerful as they said it would be. The firemen were happy, excited. Look how high the water goes, their faces were saying.

A man wanted to get his luggage off the end of the platform as the flames reached out for it. The police held him back.

"The last shirt I own in this world is in that top box," he was yelling.

"Looks like you'll be goin' to church shirtless!" shouted a man with a voice I'd heard recently. It was the pest from the streetcar who my mother had told to shut his gob.

"Maybe you'll be able to get a real good shirt this time with the insurance money!" another guy in the crowd shouted.

"And have a mind to get the shirt made by O'Reilly. That way it'll be sure to fit ya!" shouted the pest from the streetcar.

"Unless it's the wrong size!" the other answered and the crowd let out a big laugh.

"Wrong size or not, at least it won't be on fire!" shouted the pest.

"Unless O'Reilly has a fire. What'll he do then?" was the answer.

"Why, I suppose he'll wind up the way he is now— shirtless!"

"Unless they up and have a FIRE SALE at

O'Reilly's!" shouts the pest's partner. The crowd was moaning because the jokes were so bad.

"Why don't you two go and get a job on the stage up at the Grand Opera House and give us a rest!" my mother shouted and the whole crowd roared with laughter.

"Do you think it's possible," my mother said quiet to me, "to be born without a brain at all?"

I knew why my mother was speaking out and drawing attention the way she did on the streetcar and then there at the fire. She knew my father would be asking people if they'd seen his wife and kid. She was making sure they didn't miss us. People would tell my father they saw us.

He'd make them tell. Everybody was afraid of him.

The trains west and east were late leaving, of course, but they left Ottawa all the same, and we hoped that my father would believe we were on one of them.

My mother and I moved slow back to the back of the crowd, pretending to go to the trains but then pulled our collars up around our faces and circled quick back toward town and Parliament Hill.

We left the glow of the burning depot behind us. We walked past the iron gates where I saw Wilfrid Laurier go in. The sky started to lighten and we headed across Sappers' Bridge.

My mother pulled my arm and we backed up against the side of one of the bridge pillars. I followed her eyes where they stared wide at a streetcar moving past.

There were only a few people on this one, now that the rush hour was over.

It wasn't hard to spot my father sitting there in one of the center seats, staring straight ahead.

His face was twisted in rage.

He was heading for the CPR depot.

Looking for us.

5

Never Forget This Moment

DID I SAY I WAS WELL OVER A HUNDRED YEARS of age? I forget. I think I did.

Sometimes, when you're my age, your body feels so light you feel like you're going to disappear. Or you feel kind of transparent. I feel sometimes afraid that when the nurse comes in to check on me she'll be able to see right through me. I feel papery, like the skin of a long-gone bug. But I don't really think about my body most of the time. I ignore it as much as I can. I mean, what's the sense? I've spent decades feeding it, watering it, satisfying it and enough is enough.

They can come in and suck me up their vacuum cleaners for all I care.

No, now it's my mind and my mind only that I care about.

And my memory. My memory, which is like an ancient painting on the wall of a deep cave. If I carry the flaming torch into the cave, get the light shining just right, flickering just nice there in the shadows, and if I recognize and remember the symbols and the letters, the pictures and the words, well then, I can read and interpret exactly what's there.

There was the fire at the CPR depot. My mother and I pretended to get on one of the trains early that morning. Then we slipped away, spent the rest of the day hiding around town in places where we were sure we wouldn't run into my father.

Like church, for instance.

We went to morning mass at St. Brigit's and then went down to the Sisters of Charity to see if we could pick out a big warm sweater for me and maybe an extra flannel shirt out of the clothing-for-the-poor bin. We got a nice sweater and a shirt and later walked up St. Patrick Street and met Father Fortier, the priest who had baptized me. My mother and Father Fortier had a chat in private. I knew what they were talking about. My mother was telling him where she was sending me to get away from my father. And she probably told him where she was going, too, but I wasn't sure. Father Fortier knew all about our troubles. And more, probably.

I didn't like Father Fortier much because of what he did when I was baptized. See, I wasn't baptized for some reason until I was around five years old. Usually you get baptized when you're just a tiny baby about the length of your father's forearm, but for some reason I wasn't available.

But, when I finally did get baptized, Father Fortier was mad that I was so old, so he pulled my hair until I cried and told me he was doing this so I'd never forget this moment. He had a fistful of my curly hair, and was squeezing it while he put the holy water on me. The water running down my face was holy water and tears.

"I'm pulling your hair, lad, so's you'll never forget this sacred moment," he said, and then just to make sure I'd never forget that sacred moment, he banged my forehead five times against the side of the stone basin. Once for The Father. Once for The Son. Once for The Holy Ghost. And twice for *Amen*! (Once for Ah. Once for men.)

He was right.

I never did forget that sacred moment.

My mother had more money than I ever saw. She had been stealing a little bit out of my father's pants every chance she got for the last couple of months. She had almost nine dollars in coins in her bag.

We went into a drugstore on Sussex Street and looked around in there. The guy behind the counter was writing out a big ad on a piece of cardboard.

"Odorama Tooth Powder," the sign said. "A New Thing—25 cents!"

"What's that?" my mother said.

"It's a new thing," the clerk said.

"I know that," my mother said. "I can read. But what does it do?"

"You sprinkle it on a brush and scrub your teeth with it," the clerk said. "Your breath'll turn out smelling like the first rose of summer!"

"I'll take one," my mother said.

The clerk gave her a big smile and wrapped the can of tooth powder and shoved his face up close to hers, breathing all over her when she paid him the money.

"You could use a dose of it yourself!" my mother said, fanning her hand in front of her face.

My mother was what you call outspoken.

We walked up to the Oriental Cafe on the corner of Bank and Sparks. Meal tickets were seven for a dollar or fifteen cents each. "Fried oysters served with every meal!" the sign said.

We each had meat and potatoes and bread and butter and tea.

When we were finished, my mother said to the cook, "Did you forget the fried oysters, or are we havin' them for our dessert?"

When the cook started apologizing, my mother interrupted him. "Never mind," she said. "Give us an extra chunk of bread instead, and I'll put it in the boy's sack. He's goin' on a trip."

When I looked at her, wondering why she was bringing so much attention to herself when we were supposed to be on a train miles from here by now she said, "Don't worry, your father never comes near a place like this. Look around you. Do you see a sign anywhere that says 'Beer For Sale'?"

Later on that afternoon, in the Union Depot, my mother gave me the expensive tooth powder and helped me pack it and the bread in my sack. While we were stuffing the sack a porter came over to see what we were up to. My mother waved him off and we moved into a corner that was more private.

"The tooth powder is for your Uncle Ronald. There's instructions on the bottle. He's in love with the Hickey girl down the road. This will help him court her."

She hugged me and made me promise to write to her. She had tears in her eyes and hugged me again.

"You'll hear from me as soon as I figure out what we're goin' to do," she said. "Now, get on the train, get yourself a seat and wave to me out the window."

And I did that.

6

Lots of McCooeys

ON THE TRAIN I TOOK THE BOOK OUT OF THE sack that my mother had packed for me. The book was *Beautiful Joe: The Autobiography of a Dog*. The dog, Joe, telling the story of his life. The book was hard to concentrate on because you kept trying to forget about the fact that the dog could write a book. The story would be going along fine and then a little voice would interrupt your mind and say, "Just a minute. How can a dog think this stuff, say this stuff?"

In the story, a violent milkman named Jenkins slaughters a whole litter of baby pups except one. This one he cuts off the tail and the ears. I guess that's the one he liked the best. The dog's name is Beautiful Joe and gets adopted by this nice Protestant minister and his kind family. It's a story that almost makes you cry except you can't because every now and then you say to yourself, did the dog get somebody to write this for him? Then you don't feel like crying, you feel like laughing.

It was also hard to concentrate reading because of the loud conversations going on in the seats around me.

Two old guys sitting across from me were talking about a family that lived somewhere around Brennan's Hill and Low. The family's name was McCooey. The two old guys trading stories about the family of McCooeys had their window open and a lot of soot from the smokestack of the steam engine was blowing in the window. The reason they had the window open was so they could spit their tobacco juice through the window instead of on the floor.

When the train left Ottawa, they were spitting on the floor. They spit on the floor while we stopped in Hull, and then Ironside and then Farmer's Rapids and then pulling into Chelsea. While the train was taking on water at the station at Chelsea, a conductor came along and told the two old guys to quit spitting on the floor.

"Where do you think you are, at home?" he told the two old guys.

"We don't spit on the floor at home," one of the old guys said. The one with hardly any teeth.

"Well, don't do it here then," the conductor told them, "or you'll be put off the train and you can try walkin' for a while."

"Walkin' might be faster 'n you're going along, anyway," the other old guy with the big hairy ears said.

"Open the window and spit out there," the conductor said. "And try not to hit any innocent bystanders!"

So the two old guys were spitting tobacco juice out the window. But sometimes a gust of wind would take what they spit and blow it back in and give me a bit of a shower.

Me and my book by the dog, Beautiful Joe.

By the time the train pulled into Tenaga they were still talking about the McCooey family.

"Oh, they were a big gang, the McCooeys were," the guy with the hairy ears said.

"And there's lots of them left, I suppose," the guy with only a few teeth said.

"There's a few of them left," said the other old guy, squirting a big slurp of tobacco juice out the window into the wind and right back in onto the seat beside me.

"There's Walkabout McCooey, who all he does is walk all over the place all the time, winter and summer, spring and fall, rain or shine."

"And there's Peek-a-boo McCooey, who's always looking out from behind trees or rocks or posts or buildings."

"And there's Turnaround McCooey who can't take a half a dozen steps without turning completely around. If he's walking down the road to church, for instance, he'll walk for a little bit, stop, turn completely around, then continue on his way until pretty soon he'll have to stop and turn himself around again."

They were talking like this off and on while the train stopped at all the little places on the way up to Low.

Gleneagle, Kirk's Ferry, Larrimac.

Before each stop a second conductor, one with a voice like a cannon, would walk through the car, yelling out the name of each place.

"Burnet! Next stop Burnet!" he came through again, booming out the name of the next stop. Some of the passengers would tease him, saying, "Didn't we just go through Burnet back there?" This would make the huge conductor bend down and look out the windows of the train to see where we were. Then he'd yell out again, even louder this time, just to show he was right all along, "BURNET! NEXT STOP BURNET!" and make everybody screw up their faces from the pain of the noise of his awful voice.

At each stop there was a lot of shouting and blowing of steam and grinding of metal and slamming of doors. At each stop, empty metal milk cans would be thrown off and piled onto wagons along the train. And when the cars clanged together, the flesh of the horses hitched to the wagons would quiver and their tails would switch.

And there were lots of people on the platform at each station, there to meet the train. It was exciting. They would go and stand on the platform and watch. See who was coming to town, who was leaving, what kind of parcels were dropped off from Eaton's and other places.

It was exciting to meet the train every evening. You didn't need a reason. You didn't have to be picking up a parcel or meeting somebody or saying goodbye to somebody. It was just exciting to go and watch.

Sometimes you'd see people open up packs of the *Ottawa Citizen* or the *Evening Journal* and maybe look for something in the paper they wanted to see.

Sometimes you'd see somebody open up the paper and read something to a couple of other people.

After Burnet there was Chemin-des-Pins and Cascades. Often the train would run right along the Gatineau River, making the lamps sparkle and run in the darkened water.

The two old guys across from me were still trading gossip about the McCooey family.

"And then there's Shirt-tail McCooey, who wears all the shirts he owns at the same time. He has about ten shirts and in the morning he gets up and puts all of them on! And they say each day he rotates them."

"Rotates them?"

"Yes, you see the one he wore on the outside yesterday, he puts on the inside today. That way he always has a different shirt next to his skin each day and a different one on the outside each day, so he never has to wash them!"

"Patterson! Patterson, next stop!" the huge conductor boomed.

"Didn't we just leave Patterson?" somebody shouted. The conductor, who was shaped like a barrel, bent down and checked out the windows at the shadows of trees and fields sliding slowly by, just to make sure.

"PATTERSON! NEXT STOP PATTERSON!" he bellowed, and everybody in the car held their hands over their ears and laughed.

I was getting tired of hearing about the McCooeys, and I tried to get back to my book about the mutilated dog, Beautiful Joe. We stopped at Farm Point and then Rockhurst, and came into Wakefield, which was a pretty big town right on the water.

Until two years before, Wakefield was the end of the line, but now the train went all the way up to Gracefield, past Low. A brand new track.

People in Wakefield were pretty excited when the train came up from Ottawa every night because the train ran right up the main street of town. It was so close to the houses that you could see into the rooms— maybe see them having their tea or almost shake hands with them from the train window while they sat and rocked on their little verandahs after supper.

It was a mild evening for November. But this evening there was something else in Wakefield getting almost as much attention as the train.

In a large express wagon pulled by four horses there were six policemen and some other men following in another big express wagon also being pulled by two teams of powerful horses. As they passed under the streetlamps I could see it was the same six policemen my mother and I saw that morning on the street in Ottawa. The sides of the express wagons were down so everybody could see the shiny, knee-length boots, the spotless blue uniforms and the twinkling gold buttons.

And the tall, fancy, strange-looking hats with the feather plumes and chin straps with tassels.

And their revolvers in the shiny black holsters on their broad belts.

You could tell the way people were watching the two teams of four trotting by, hauling these strange-looking policemen and other official-looking gents, that nobody knew who they were or where they were going.

One thing was sure, they weren't staying in Wakefield. They were heading north.

"They won't be doing any trotting once they leave Wakefield," one man who was passing up the aisle was saying. "The roads above here are knee-deep in mud!"

After Wakefield things got a lot quieter and darker. The little stations at Alcove and Lordsvale had hardly any light.

The two across from me were still talking about the McCooeys.

"And there's still lots of others. Whistle McCooey, who whistles all the time, even in his sleep, they say; and Barnyard McCooey, who can imitate all the animals on the farm; and Mean Bone McCooey, who fights all the time."

And then the other one: "And Mouthwash McCooey, who swears all the time, even though his old mother washes his mouth out with homemade soap every night; and Sobbing McCooey, who cries all the time, even when he's laughing; and Nosey McCooey, who smells everything (he'll smell your shoulder if you stop to talk to him on the road); and Ahem McCooey (she says "Ahem" after every second or third word); and Boner McCooey, well, we don't have to point out how *he* goes around all the time!"

They were running out of McCooey stories and one of the men, the one without very many teeth, was dozing off. The one with the hairy ears was trying to explain about Tommy Twelve Toes McCooey, who had six toes on each foot and could outrun a deer...

But there was another conversation further up the aisle that floated into my ears, blocking everything else out. I put my book back in my sack and acted like I was ready to get off the train.

I stood up and stretched and picked up my coat and sack and moved up toward the end of the coach and sat down again. There were quite a few empty seats since we left Wakefield. A man and a woman were talking. The man was eating an onion.

The train wheels clicked and the engine chuffed and the trees and rocks echoed by. We pulled in and out of Brennan's Hill hardly seeing anybody and only one light.

I listened to the gossips speaking quietly.

"Yes, and the two women, twins they are, identical, brought the bailiff into the kitchen, sat him down at the table with a cuppa tea and got around behind him and one of the identical twins—nobody knows which one of course because they're both so exactly the same— one of them brained him a good one with a porcelain pisspot on the back of the head and knocked him silly. Then the twins, they opened the trap to the cellar and rolled him down in there and he spent two days or more down there before they let him out and sent him down the road and told him not to come back...

"A bailiff named Flatters it was. Shot dead as a doornail outside his house in Aylmer only a few weeks later."

"Was it the twins that done it, that shot him?" said the man with the mouthful of onion.

"That's what they say," said the woman. "That's what they say."

"The O'Malley girls, is it? Is that what they're called?" asked the onion man.

"I believe it is," said the woman. "Yes, the O'Malley girls is what they call them, I believe. Shot him dead outside his own house."

"Quite the girls they must be, them O'Malley girls."

"Yes, they must, they must indeed!"

Could that be right? I thought. My mother's second cousins once removed, the O'Malley girls? The cousins I had the sugar and tea and candy in my sack for? Murderers? Couldn't be. Must be some other people with the same name. But identical twins? How many identical twins could there be around named O'Malley?

"LOW! NEXT STOP LOW!" the huge conductor roared right behind me, making the hair on the back of my neck stand straight out while the train let out a bellowing, lonely cry that echoed again and again from the oldest mountains in the world.

7

A Bed of Thistles

THE HEADLAMPS OF THE STEAM ENGINE TRIED to stab into the dark forest but they couldn't. There was no moon but the sky was clear and if you shaded your eyes with your hands you could see some stars.

There were lanterns at each end of the platform and other lights moving around in the gloom. Parcels and mailbags and cream cans were being loaded onto wagons and some men were throwing short logs into the car behind the engine.

There were smells of burning wood, sawdust, spruce gum, horses, leather, milk, plums.

It was a nice night for November, not cold, but you could feel, every little while, a small burst of Arctic air, just a warning that it was coming. Winter. First Thanksgiving, then winter.

Shadow shapes were working, moving around, laughing, shouting in the half light of the Low station.

The train let go a giant sneeze and started moving with a grinding shudder.

Conversations were going back and forward.

"Lovely and mild?" somebody said.

"It is that," said somebody else.

"Little wetter than last fall," somebody added.

"Quite a bit wetter," another agreed.

"You know it's going to snow any day now!" shouted a man from the other end of the platform.

"We know that!" another one said from on top of a wagon.

"Then it will be winter for sure!" yelled the first.

"We know that, too!" roared the other.

"And then, spring!" the first kept on.

"We know all this. Why are you telling us these things that we already know?"

"Just reminding you is all. Just to make sure you're up to date!"

Soon the train howled away up the track into the bush and around a bend, and the little light on the caboose twinkled into the trees and disappeared.

The station was sudden quiet. Most of the people seemed to fade into the night as fast as the train did. The train left and sucked the life right out of the station with it.

Except for one shape, standing off to the side in the flickering light of the lantern at the end of the platform. In the shadows beside him, his horse and rig.

It was the first time I ever met my Uncle Ronald. And the first word I ever heard my Uncle Ronald say was my name.

"Mickey," he said, the name rumbling deep out of his broad chest. "I've come to meet ya." I loved the sound of my name, the way it came out from inside him.

He took my bag from me with two fingers. At first he looked to be about as tall as my father but then I realized he was standing down on the second step up to the platform. When I stepped down beside him I was standing beside a giant.

In the mostly darkness he was there.

He helped me up into the little rig and then got in himself. When he put his weight on it the springs sagged and groaned. There was a little dark-lamp on a hook behind him.

"This is Second Chance Lance," he said gently, introducing me to his horse. "He's very intelligent. Aren't you, Lance?" Lance's left ear twitched as he began pulling us out of the station yard. Soon we were in the complete dark. Uncle Ronald closed the shutter on the dark-lamp and cut off the shaft of light.

"See more with that out," he said, and Lance broke into a trot. "Once your eyes get used to the dark."

The stars showed the line of trees, and Lance's hooves thudded soft on the grassy road.

"The main road is mainly mud," said Uncle Ronald, "but these side roads are fine."

We passed slow some open fields and a winking farmhouse light or two.

We rounded a bend along a fence and Lance slowed down to a walk while Uncle Ronald whispered to him, "Sh, sh, sh." We stopped without a sound and Uncle Ronald put his huge hand on top of my head and turned it to the side and pointed with his other arm where I should look.

"Look there!" he whispered. I looked down his arm where he was pointing. All I could make out was a fence and a clearing. Uncle Ronald snapped the shutter of the dark-lamp open and sent a shaft of light toward where we were looking.

Two big round yellow eyes.

A complete white feather coat covering everything, feet and all.

A snowy owl.

"Arrived yesterday," Uncle Ronald said and slid shut the lantern. "He's early. Beautiful creature. Powerful. Won't say a word, though. Will he, Lance? We tried on our way over to meet you to get him to talk. Not a word out of him."

Lance seemed to know that there was no use hanging around to hear the snowy owl say "hoo,"so we took off again, thumping softly up the road. The rig swinging smooth along.

"I had a letter from me sister. You'll stay with us for a while." A long pause. "Or longer, we'll see." I hadn't yet seen Uncle Ronald's face. It was mostly his voice that made me feel so safe.

I wondered what she told him in the letter. Did she tell him she was stealing money from my father's pants? Did she say she thought of axing his throat? Did she tell about the belt and the fear? Did she say about me and my problem with beds? Did she say in the letter my father wanted to kill us?

"I know your father," he said.

I waited. Waited for him to say more. But he didn't.

The soft thudding of Lance's hooves on the grass stirred something along the road, making a loud buzzing whirring clatter. Lance answered with a short whinny of his own.

"Never mind those partridge, Lance. You leave them alone. They need their rest."

One farmhouse we passed had a flickering lamp on in an upstairs window. The curtain was drawn but I saw the shadow of a figure moving several times.

Uncle Ronald looked up at the window as soon as it

came into view and kept his eyes on it until he was twisted almost right around in his seat.

I wondered who lived there who he was so interested in.

A stream bubbled alongside us in the dark as we drove.

We turned into a side road that was even softer and quieter. We stopped. We were at a closed gate. Lance lifted the wooden latch with his nose. He bunted the gate with his head and pulled us through. Behind us, I heard the gate swing shut and heard the wooden latch fall back into the notch.

"That top hinge needs a little oil, doesn't it, Lance?"

The next gate was the same.

We slid quiet past some buildings looming alongside and then pulled up to a stop. Lance let out a pleasant little sigh and a short neigh in his throat. Glad to be home.

The door opened and a woman in a long dress and an apron raised a lamp for us.

"Come in, young Mickey, ya poor thing. You'll come in and sit down and have a plate and a cup..."

Uncle Ronald disappeared with Lance and I went into the kitchen. At the stove was another woman, in the same long dress and the same apron.

"Come in, young Mickey, ya poor thing. Sit down there and there'll be a plate and a cup in front of ya quick as a wink!"

It was the O'Malley girls!

Uncle Ronald came in. "This is Edith and Mildred O'Malley, Mickey," he said, but he didn't say which was which or who was who. This was the first look at him I had in the light.

His eyes were big and dark and his hair was black and curly and hung over his broad forehead and partly over his ears. He was as tall as the door, and his shoulders were broad and sloping from his muscled neck. He wore a great belt round his middle with a tail hanging down on each side. When he took off his jacket his chest pulled and strained the buttons of his shirt. His wrists were wide and his hands strong and veined. His thighs filled out his pants and his boots were round in the toe and wide in the heel.

He was big and powerful but looked soft and gentle at the same time.

After a little snack of fried pork and bread and butter and tea and a lot of fuss, I unpacked my bag.

While I placed the things from my bag on the table, the O'Malley girls stood behind me. I was pretty tense at first, sitting there at the table. Was this where the bailiff was sitting when he got knocked silly with the porcelain pot?

I put the pencil and pad out.

"I'm to write my mother a letter every Sunday," I said.

"We'll remind you," the O'Malley girls said, both at the same time.

I put out the cake of soap and the towel and the O'Malley girls showed me where the washstand with the basin and the jug was.

To each item I put on the table—the socks, the mitts, the shirt, scarf, toque—the O'Malley girls said "mmm" or "good" or "grand."

To the clinking envelope with the seventy-five cents in it they said, "He has his own money," and to the bottle of Skiel Cod Liver Oil they read the label, "For plump cheeks," both together like a little song.

To the book, *Beautiful Joe* by Margaret Marshall Saunders but really told by the dog, they said, "Hard to believe, a dog writing a book!"

To the tea and the sugar and the candy, they said, "How thoughtful of your mother, she didn't need to..."

But the hit of the unpacking was the can of Odorama Tooth Powder. Uncle Ronald was sitting with his chair leaned back against the wall next to the chimney.

I echoed my mother's words.

"This tooth powder is for Uncle Ronald to help him court the Hickey girl down the road," I said.

"Indeed!" said one of the O'Malley girls and then they both laughed quietly the very same way. Uncle Ronald's chair hit the floor with a thud. He was laughing too but his face was a little red.

Time to sleep.

They put me in a little narrow bed in the space under the stairs. They sent Uncle Ronald out to the barn to make my mattress.

"He'll have the trundle bed under the stairs," one of the O'Malley girls said. "Fill that sack with fresh straw, Ronald, and he'll be as snug as a bug in a rug, as they say!"

The sack was sewn out of unstitched flour bags and then filled with straw and hay.

"Put some clover in, too, Ronald, so's it will smell real nice," the other O'Malley girl called softly as Uncle Ronald left with the big sack.

"And try not, Ronald, to put too many thistles in

with it!" one of them said, and they both gave me a big wink at the same time.

"Thistles sticking in your back, Mickey, have a way of keeping you awake all night!" one of them said.

"That's the truth, Mickey," said the other one.

Maybe it would be a good idea to be awake all night, I thought, filling up with disgust for myself.

"Maybe you should fill it up just with thistles," I said, feeling pretty sorry for myself.

They both gave me a question-mark smile. The same, exact same little smile. I wondered if they knew what I meant.

The O'Malley girls had curly red hair, freckles, brown eyes. They spoke their words very clearly. They always said your name when they said anything to you. They would often touch you when they talked to you. Always had a sweet smile for you. Small, even teeth. Pudgy arms. Small hard hands. Walked and worked around the house making almost no noise. Very neat. Everything in the right place.

Each wore a small crucifix cross on a little chain around her throat.

I went to bed and lay squeezed as close to the wall as I could.

The lamp moved up the stairs over me and shadows danced and light slid and ran and winked and then it was dark.

I dreaded going to sleep.

But I went, anyway.

8

Uncle Ronald Beats the Rooster

IT TOOK ME A LONG TIME TO FIGURE OUT where I was.

I knew one thing for sure. There was something sharp sticking in my back.

And the sloping structure above me was creaking and stretching and sagging and through the cracks a shimmering flame moved down.

And there were heavy tiptoed footsteps.

And something enormous was on its way down from somewhere to harm me. Something raging and dangerous descending to me, going to smash me flat.

Half asleep still.

I was buried alive under something somewhere and my father was coming down to finish me off.

But then, what was sticking in my back was cleaning out my brain and blowing away the fog of terror.

I was in my Uncle Ronald's farmhouse sleeping under his stairs and the thing sticking in my back was probably one of his thistles. And the bag of rage coming down was only Uncle Ronald making his way as quiet as he could down the staircase.

Then the dancing flame of another gliding coal-oil lamp showed two shadows, two figures exactly the same shape along the wall. The O'Malley girls.

I heard Uncle Ronald go out the door and the O'Malley girls moving around the kitchen, clanking metal. Then I heard Second Chance Lance outside snorting and then Uncle Ronald came back in and then the O'Malley girls went out and got in the rig and Lance thumped away.

Then Uncle Ronald crept by me and went back up to bed without using a lamp, as quiet as he could, making the stairs groan in pain from his weight.

And then I heard the spring of his bed grind down, heard him sigh. A big sigh and then silence.

My mattress was dry so I thought I couldn't have been asleep that long.

I began planning how I would get up in a minute without banging my head on the stairs. I planned how to find my way in the dark to the door.

I felt warm and safe while making these plans because Uncle Ronald was there in the house right above me.

I planned how to open the door and slip out onto the cold grass in my bare feet. I planned to piss, come back, find the bed, get back in, move the thistle.

While I was making all these careful, big plans I fell asleep again.

When you wake up on a farm, it's supposed to be the rooster who wakes you up. It wasn't the rooster, though, this time, on my first morning on this farm. It was Uncle Ronald. Uncle Ronald was up long before the rooster ever even took it into his tiny brain to open one of his sharp little eyes and give a cock-a-doodle-do.

The first thing a person does in the morning is listen. Some people hear birds, some hear bombs, some hear alarm-clock radios, some hear thunder, some hear the breathing of somebody loved, some hear silence.

48

But my sound, the sound that I heard that morning, was Uncle Ronald. Of all the sounds I ever loved from any time of the day or night—the sound of a fly buzzing on the dining-room window on Sunday afternoon, the sound the metal would make when you clipped Lance's harness to the ring or his trace to his whippletree, the sound a calf makes when its nose is halfway into a pail of milk, the sound of the knives of the mower over on the next field, the sound the workhorse makes when she's headed for the well after a long hot day, the sound of the whip-poor-will at night, the sound of sleet against the kitchen window when you're warm inside the house, the sound of lightning and the sound of thunder, the sound of the ax splitting a stick of hard ash, the sound of the ticking clock, the sound of the dog snoring behind the stove, the sound of the ice breaking up on the river in the spring, the sound of the summer breeze in the white pines, the sound of the rooster and the bull, the heat bug in August, the gooseberries hitting the bottom of the pail, the sound of blowing out the lamp—of all these sounds I've loved, I love best the memory of the sound of Uncle Ronald in the morning.

First he'd go downstairs in his sock feet so as not to wake anybody up. When Uncle Ronald put on his first boot he'd stamp it and stomp it on the kitchen floor. He'd be making sure that his foot was at the very bottom of the boot, making sure that the bottom of his foot and his boot were tight together for the rest of the day. He'd slam the heel of the boot into the kitchen floor right on top of the trap door that went into the cellar where he always stood. The cellar where the

O'Malley girls once put the tax collector. Then he'd slam the ball of his foot onto the trap door that went into the cellar to make sure his toes were well fixed into the toe of his boot. Then he'd bang the whole boot, thundering his full weight into the boot on top of the cellar door, turning the whole house into a huge drum.

Then he'd do his other boot.

Then, once my Uncle Ronald had his boots well on, he'd start to get ready to wash his face. You could hear him clanging the dipper against the water pail and then you knew he was filling the basin with just the right amount.

Then you could hear Uncle Ronald begin to growl and you knew he had his hands in the icy water in the basin and you knew that any second now you'd hear him howling in pain when he cupped the water in his hands and drove it into his face. He would force the icy water into his face like a crazy man smashing himself in the face with a board. Once he got by the first water shock, Uncle Ronald would grab the bar of soap and begin trying to rub his whole face off with both his hands. While he was doing this he would make blubbering, spitting, slobbering, bubbling, coughing, snorting, sucking, choking sounds—sounds like you would hear if you were hearing a man drowning in something thick, like pudding.

After Uncle Ronald was done with his face he'd unbutton his long underwear to the waist and grab the face rag and do his neck and his chest and then under his arms, which was the worst, coldest part. While he was doing this part of himself he would make a sound like you hear today ambulances and police cars making. *Woop! Woop! Woop! Woop! Woop!*

Now Uncle Ronald was finished washing and was putting his underwear top back on and his big shirt, sighing the whole time, sighing and grunting and clearing his throat and making other sounds that he made when he was happy like sniffing and coughing and growling and smacking his lips and blowing puffs of breath out his nose with a grunt, like boxers do when getting in shape for a fight, punching a large bag in a gym.

Now Uncle Ronald was ready to put the kettle on.

First he cut kindling.

Beside the stove was a woodbox.

Beside the woodbox a small block.

Uncle Ronald had a short piece of rough lumber maybe left over from when he built the new barn the year before, in 1894.

Around the time the track was finished and the first train came up to Low.

Uncle Ronald cut kindling the way you see cooks on TV cut celery or mushrooms. He would have that piece of lumber end cut into about a dozen strips exactly the same width in less time than it would take one of those cooks on TV to slice up a bunch of celery. The second last strip to be cut would spring away right beside Uncle Ronald's big finger that was holding up what was to be the last strip.

Then Uncle Ronald would sink the small ax back into the block with one lightning-strong flip of his wrist and the blade of the ax so deep that he was the only one who would be able to pull it out again.

Then Uncle Ronald would start banging and clanging and ringing the stove. He'd shake the grate, slam the crank back on the hook, hit the draft back and forward, lift the iron lids and bang them down, open the door, kick it closed, pick wood out of the box, throw it back, pick other wood, open the door again, kick it shut, ring the metal ashes shovel, kick closed the ash box, drop the lifter onto the floor, rattle the poker, twist and squeal the rusty spring of the damper, ding and ring and dong the iron frying pan and smash the kettle onto the stove top three times, just to make sure it knew who was the boss.

And it was somewhere during all this friendly racket that lying there I made a discovery that filled me with wonder and joy.

My mattress was dry.

I had not pissed the bed!

Then I heard the rooster crow.

Too late, mister rooster!

Uncle Ronald beat you to it!

9

Policemen's Nuts

THE FIRE IN THE STOVE SOUNDED LIKE CLOTHES snapping and whooshing on a clothesline in a big wind.

"The O'Malley girls won't be down for breakfast this morning," Uncle Ronald told me as he buttered a hot thick piece of almost burnt toast for me. "They had to go out in the middle of the night to do some work and they're pretty played out."

"I heard them," I said. "I heard them go out." I waited to see if he was going to tell me where they went, what they were doing.

Uncle Ronald poured me a cup of hot tea and moved the heavy pitcher of cream over closer to me, pushing it across the table with one finger.

I waited a little longer.

Uncle Ronald plopped a ladle of porridge in a bowl in front of me and gave me a spoon and showed me that the brown sugar was in a big tin on the table.

"The sugar's hard in the tin. You'll have to hit it on the side of the table a few times to loosen some up fer yerself."

He wasn't going to tell me.

"Where were the O'Malley girls going?" I said.

"Yep," said Uncle Ronald. "Pretty tired they were when they got back. I checked on them a while ago. Sound asleep the two of them in their bed together. Just as quiet as two spoons in a drawer."

Uncle Ronald flipped over two pancakes in a pan on

the stove and shoved some more wood in and kicked the hot iron door shut. He went to the pantry and got out a big sticky jar of maple syrup. Not telling me.

"Good year last spring for the syrup," he said softly, as though it was some kind of a secret. "I've got twenty of the best maples in the Gatineau. Just look at them and they'll offer up their sap to ya."

I wondered if he bothered to tap the trees to get the syrup, or did he just pet them and whisper to them and squeeze them?

"What were the O'Malley girls doing last night?" I asked. Uncle Ronald poured thick cream on my porridge from a white jug.

"Do you like cream on your porridge?" he asked.

Not going to tell me.

He filled a big kettle from a pail and set it on the back of the stove.

"After breakfast I'll show you how we get water," he said.

"Some men on the train said stuff about the O'Malley girls," I said.

"The well is at the bottom of the cliff out there. We have a winch so you can get the pail of water up without havin' to go down there yourself. I'll show you how to work it after your breakfast."

I was about to give up when Uncle Ronald whispered in my face while shoving a plate of pancakes in front of me, dousing them with butter and covering them with syrup.

"Can you keep a secret?" he whispered.

"Yes," I whispered back. "Yes I can."

"Well, here it is, then. The O'Malley girls, they were out late last night removing some policemen's nuts!"

10

Second Chance for Lance

THERE WAS NO MORE TALK ABOUT THE O'Malley girls.

Uncle Ronald showed me how to get water.

From the house a clay path led through a small potato field to the edge of a cliff about three stories high.

There was a short wood pier at the top of the cliff, held there by heavy rocks eleven hundred million years old.

A heavy tight wire ran from the pier down the cliff into the clear sparkling well water. There was a crank that turned a drum that wound up a long rope that was attached to a little pulley wheel and a snap hook.

You snapped the pail to the hook, let the pail run down the wire on the pulley wheel until it hit the well water. Then you waited until the pail filled up with water and sank out of sight.

Then you started to turn the crank, pulling the pail up the wire to where you were. Then you unhooked the full pail—careful don't spill any—and set it down.

Now you did it all over again with the second pail.

Now you had two full pails of beautiful water to carry back to the house. Two pails were better to carry than one because you were balanced and it was easier to walk.

Uncle Ronald carried two.

I carried two.

Back in the house, Uncle Ronald piled all the breakfast dishes into a tub and was pouring boiling water over them when there was a heavy pounding on the door.

"That'll be Even Steven," Uncle Ronald said. "Open the door for him before he breaks it down!"

I opened the door and a short man as wide as a stove took my hand and shook it.

"This is me sister's boy," Uncle Ronald told him. "Come to stay with us for a while. You sit down, Steven, and talk to him, while I go out and milk the cows. The O'Malley girls are tired and won't be down until later. The tea's still warm in the pot."

Even Steven's hand felt like a big knot in a pine log.

He started talking as he poured his tea.

"Big doin's in town," he said. "Policemen in funny-looking hats. Here for the taxes no doubt. Big wagons. Stayed overnight at Brooks' Hotel. Came in late. Sneaked in. Didn't take the train you were on. Came in like thieves in the stealth of the night!"

I wanted to tell him that only yesterday I saw policemen something like that—once in Ottawa, once in Wakefield—but Even Steven kept talking.

"Did Ronnie tell you what happened to the last tax collectors that came around here? He didn't? Get one of the O'Malley girls to tell you what happened. Edith or Mildred, it wouldn't matter which one. They both tell it well.

"One of them was alone in the house that day. Her sister was out in the chicken coop and her cousin Ronald was in the far field and at the door is this bailiff calling himself Bailiff Flatters. Shows her his badge. She brings him in and sits him at the table and him polite as anything—an average-size fella, clean shaven, wearing a suit, lot of papers in a satchel—puts on his spectacles, gets out a pencil, goin' down a list of names, tellin' her all the while what the O'Malleys owe and how much in arrears and how many years back it's been, and now he's not as polite as he was but she's being very polite, puttin' on the tea for him and tellin' him about how her father came over in '47 without a shirt on his back, leavin' the old country because he was hounded by the likes of this and what were taxes for anyway, what did the government ever do for us up here when we wanted decent roads and a school? While she was explainin' this to him he says that her father had no business settling on this land and that they didn't even have any legal title to it and that her father was only what they called a squatter. A squatter! That made her blood boil! Insulting the name of her poor ol' father, God Rest His Soul in Heaven, callin' him a squatter if you please! Just then, her eyes fell on the piss pot which was sittin' on the bench beside the stove (she'd just emptied it when he came knockin'), and she grabbed it by the handle (it was their best one, the heavy one, the porcelain with the big roses embossed around the rim), and she swung it round and she brained him with it, hit him a dandy across the side of the head just as her sister, Edith, or was it Mildred, came in with the eggs. Then they pulled up the cellar door—that one right there—and the two of them they rolled your Mister Bailiff Flatters down into the darkness down there! You could say she *flattened* your

Mister Flatters. Squatter! You can squat down there for a while, Mr. Taxman! they told him.

"Everybody loves hearing the story, specially the part about the roses around the rim of the pot," Even Steven said.

"I'll bet his head was ringing for a week after that!" he laughed. "Kept him there two days! A year or so later somebody shot the man in front of his house way over in Aylmer. Wasn't the O'Malley girls though. They've never been to Aylmer. Low is as far as they've ever been in their whole lives. Everybody says they did it though. That's good, don't you think? To have a reputation like that? I wish they'd all say that I went and shot him!"

It was hard to see where Even Steven stopped to take a breath. He could store a lot of volume of air in that stove of a chest of his. Good for talking for a long time without taking a breath!

"Soon your Uncle Ronnie will be back in and we'll hitch up Second Chance Lance and skip into town and see what the soldiers in the funny hats are going to try to do to us. Lance'll get us there in no time flat. Did your uncle tell you about Lance? How he got him. He didn't? How old Mean Bone McCooey was skidding a big stick of square timber up his steep road on Dizzy Peak with little Lance there—Lance a way too small for that job. Every time poor little Lance'd get the weight partway up the slope it'd get too much for him and back down he'd slide. This was a big joke to Ol' Mean Bone. Ol' Mean Bone was sayin', 'This is your last chance, Lance,' and started callin' him Last Chance Lance just to get a big laugh from all the lads standin' around watchin'. And your Uncle Ronald, he was there, and he got to feelin' real sorry for the little horse so he offered to buy Lance right there on the spot—offered him a litter of piglets and a hardly used crosscut saw—but Ol' Mean Bone, he wouldn't hear of it. He wanted that little horse to pull that heavy piece of square timber up that steep slope or perish tryin'! Then, your Uncle Ronnie, he made a bet with Ol' Mean Bone. Bet him the price of the horse that he could get Lance up the hill with that load, first try. If he could, he'd get to keep the horse. If he couldn't, he'd give him the pigs and the saw and go home empty-handed. 'I'll take that chance,' says Mean Bone, and the bet was on. 'One condition,' says your Uncle Ronnie. 'You'll have to turn your back on us until it's over.' Why is that?' says Mean Bone. 'Because I think it's your ugly face that's keeping this horse from doing his best on this job,' says your Uncle Ronnie. Well, everybody laughed and Ol' Mean Bone laughed too and turned his back and said, 'Go ahead, do your best you two, for it won't be long that I'll have meself a nice litter of pigs and a crosscut saw hardly used, and you'll be goin' home empty-handed!'"

It was hard to concentrate on Even Steven's story because he didn't seem to be breathing. And the longer he didn't breathe, the higher his voice got.

"Well, it didn't take your Uncle Ronnie long to win the bet. With Mean Bone's back turned, Ronnie tied a strong rope round his *own* waist and cinched it to Lance's horse collar and dragged both horse and timber up the top of Dizzy Peak with everybody cheering and hanging on to Mean Bone so he couldn't turn around and see what was happening!"

As Even Steven was finishing the story about how Uncle Ronald called the horse Second Chance instead of Last Chance, I was thinking how lucky Lance was to have somebody like Uncle Ronald, so strong and yet so kind, to be his master.

Just then, while Even Steven at last took a breath, Uncle Ronald came in from the milking.

"Let's hitch up Second Chance Lance and go to town," he said softly. "See what those policemen in the funny hats are up to."

11

This Wonderful Thing

IT WAS STILL PRETTY EARLY IN THE MORNING when Second Chance Lance and Even Steven and Uncle Ronald and I got to the first gate. Lance could only open the gates one way because they only swung one way. So on the way out the road a human had to open the gate and hold it open while the rig went through.

While Even Steven was opening the first gate Uncle Ronald started to tell me how Steven got his name.

"Steven talks a lot and knows just about everything about everybody, but now and then there are some things that are so secret that..."

We were through the gate now and Even Steven got back in the rig, so Uncle Ronald stopped what he was saying.

He finished it while Even Steven was off opening the second gate.

"...but now and then there are some things that are so secret that people around here often say, 'And Even Steven didn't know about that one!' For instance, what I said about the policemen's nuts? Even Steven doesn't know about that one! At least not yet, anyway!"

Even Steven climbed back in and we thumped on down the grassy road.

I was feeling kind of privileged.

I knew that the O'Malley girls probably weren't murderers. I knew how Second Chance Lance got his name and why everybody called Steven Even Steven. And I *practically* knew a secret that Even Steven didn't know, though I didn't know the whole thing just yet.

The second farmhouse on the left side of the road had curved railings around a big verandah and apple trees in the front yard with a few dead apples giving off the last smell of fall. The way Uncle Ronald was looking up at a second-floor window made me realize it was the same house last night he looked so long at.

He looked long again at the window.

Even Steven looked at me and winked a big wink. He knew something I didn't know. It was one of those big winks where you use your jaw, your cheek, your whole face. And you have to give your head a big nod downward as you do the wink.

Try it sometime. But be careful you don't hurt yourself!

Even Steven pointed off the road the other way to a little crooked house built on some rock in under the bare trees.

"That's where Jimmy Smith used to live. He's famous. First person ever to be killed by the Gatineau train! We're very proud of our Jimmy. Three or four have been killed since, but you never forget the first one. Track's only been through here two or three years now. Cut him up into twenty or more pieces! His name is known all the way from Ottawa to Gracefield."

I started to get the idea that Even Steven wanted to be famous. Wanted his own name to be known up and down the Gatineau Valley.

A little later, Uncle Ronald pointed to a big brown bird taking off with slow wing beat from a steep cliff. It screamed at Lance and us, *Ke-a, ke-a, ke-a!*

"Gyrfalcon," Uncle Ronald told me. "Makes its nest out of the bones of its prey."

In the town of Low, people were finishing their breakfast. There was smoke from every chimney and mist on every window. People were out pumping water and carrying wood and emptying pans.

Lance pulled us through the mud past the train station to Brooks' Hotel. There was a little crowd bunched around in front of the big hotel verandah.

The smell of breakfast was wrapped around the hotel like a fuzzy, thick scarf.

Some people in the crowd were teasing the two men hitching up teams of horses to the wagons.

"How much are they payin' you, Paddy?" says one farmer.

"Enough," says Paddy. "A free breakfast!"

"Enough to pay your taxes, Paddy?"

"If they'd like the breakfast back," says Paddy, "they can have it when I'm through with it, which won't be long now the way I'm feeling!"

Everybody laughed.

Each heavy horse was twice as big as Second Chance Lance and they had eight of them—four for each wagon.

They were getting ready to pull some pretty heavy loads.

All of a sudden the double doors to Brooks' Hotel opened and six policemen with shiny boots and funny hats and revolvers came out and lined up on Brooks' big wooden verandah. The same ones I'd seen early yesterday morning in Ottawa and last night in Wakefield.

The crowd was getting bigger and the rumors were going around.

"They're going to collect money," said one big farmer. "Money they say people owe in taxes. Well, they won't get any money at my place. There is no money at my place! You can't get blood out of a turnip!"

"No, but they can put your best cow into one of those big wagons there instead of the money and then what'll you do?" said another man wearing a hat that was pulled down over his ears.

"What if they can't find my best cow?" said the big farmer.

"Well, then, I suppose in a case like that they won't be able to put it in one of those fancy big wagons, will they?" said the man, pulling his hat off and bowing a big bow to the crowd, making everybody laugh.

"They won't find *my* very best cow," shouted another farmer with a voice like a goat, from the back of the crowd.

"Why is that, Johnny?" came the question from the man with the hat off.

"Because *all* my cows are my very best cows!" answered the goat voice, and the man with the hat bowed for him and got a big cheer.

I was thinking if my mother was there, she'd tell them all to go down to the nearest stage and open up a comedy show.

And shut your gobs!

Uncle Ronald wasn't laughing with the rest. He wasn't looking serious either. He looked like he was just taking it all in—understanding it all. Maybe thinking about something else, something deeper.

Soon the sergeant was done drilling his men and getting them all checked out and then they were ordered to march off the verandah and board their wagons.

They were looking pretty shiny and clean and had to be careful getting on board because the wagons were parked in an extra big pool of mud.

The bailiffs and the lawyers in their suits were already on the other wagon and things were ready to take off.

The chief bailiff was checking over a long sheet of paper where there was listed the names of all the people who owed taxes, which was everybody.

The wagons began to move.

The muscles of the haunches of the powerful horses bunched and moved under the smooth skin like engines.

What could the townspeople of Low do against such power?

The horses drew the express wagons, towing them easily and powerfully through the mud.

All of a sudden the front wheel of the second wagon took a crazy angle, then wobbled the opposite way, and the wagon dipped forward and dumped the bailiff headfirst into the road. When a wagon loses a wheel, horses don't like it, and they begin to panic. As the rear wheels folded in and dropped off, the teams shied violent to the side, whipping the wagon so the rest of the guys in the fancy clothes slid off the rear of the deck into the mud.

The same thing was happening to the policemen's wagon, only the opposite. One rear wheel went first, dumping the police against the back rack of the wagon. Then the front wheels fell right off, digging the front of the wagon deck deep into the clay and mud. The powerful horses were in a gallop, so when the front caught, the police were catapulted into the air and had quite a ride in space before they landed and slid along the road into the mucky ditch, the liquid mud.

The crowd was in a joyful mood. Singing and dancing and laughing. A free show!

The wheels fell off the wagons—somebody removed the nuts that held the wheels on! The policemen's nuts!

"I wonder was it the O'Malley girls?" said Even Steven to me and Uncle Ronald. I looked at Uncle Ronald. He showed nothing.

"I wonder if people will say it's the O'Malley girls who did this wonderful thing!" said Even Steven. His face glowed with excitement.

"Maybe people will start sayin' *you* did it, Steven!" Uncle Ronald said.

"Maybe they will!" Even Steven said, hoping.

12

Wild Geese and False Teeth

FOR THE REST OF THE MORNING THE TAX collectors were trying to get somebody to help them find new nuts for the wheels for their wagons, but nobody knew where you could find anything like that.

"Nuts? Nuts for wagon wheels? We don't think there's any nuts around this part of the country. Not for wagon wheels, anyway. There's other kinds of nuts around though!" the people were telling the bailiff and the lawyers and the policemen after they got out of the mud and got back up on the verandah at Brooks' Hotel.

"There was a nut come up around here a few years back but somebody shot him!" somebody shouted.

"The squirrels have hid all the nuts by now," shouted another funny farmer. "Come back in the spring. We'll get them to dig some up fer ya!"

Then the bailiff started asking everybody if anybody had a wagon they could lend to the tax collectors.

Nobody knew of anybody who would lend them a wagon.

Did anybody know of anybody who might *rent* the tax collectors a wagon or two for a couple of days?

Nobody did.

"I had a wagon once, but the wheels fell off!" shouted the guy with the hat over his ears, and everybody laughed.

Later, the tax collectors decided to walk around to some of the houses in the town and collect some taxes and they started asking people if they knew where so-and-so lived and where such-and-such lived. They were reading names from a list.

"Can anyone here lead us to the residence of Mr. John Egan?" the bailiff called out.

Silence.

"Can anybody here tell us where Patrick Hayes lives?"

Nobody could.

"Is there a Patrick Flynn residing in this area?"

Nobody ever heard of him.

"Does anyone here know a Michael Doyle?"

Nobody did.

"William Gleason?"

Silence.

After about ten more names, the bailiff lifted up his hands and looked up at the gray, dark sky. It was hopeless.

Then the guy with the goat voice shouted, "Maybe it would help if you went over the names again. Why don't you give it a try?"

The bailiff looked suspicious but then started the list over again. "John Egan?" Silence. "Patrick Hayes?" No answer. "Patrick Flynn? Michael Doyle?" Nothing. "William Gleason?"

"No," goat voice said. "I guess it doesn't help going over the names again after all!"

Everybody roared.

People were just starting to get bored with this game when along came Father Foley in his neat little rig.

He talked for a while to the head bailiff and made some kind of a deal with him. If they left the policemen on the verandah of Brooks' Hotel, he'd show the bailiff where some of the people lived.

The crowd got a little disgusted and broke up and drifted away.

We found out later that at the first place the bailiff knocked on the door, somebody poured boiling water on him from an upstairs window.

Even Steven stayed in town to see what was going to happen, and Uncle Ronald and Lance and I left for home.

On the way we stopped to watch a V of geese heading south.

"They've been practicing for about a month," Uncle Ronald said. "At first they did nothing but argue about how to get into the V and who was going to be the leader. Squawking and honking and crashing into each other, feathers flying."

He went quiet and we listened and watched. Uncle Ronald and I, both our faces to the sky. The V of geese was very high but you could hear them away up there, jabbering away, excited to be moving at last. Happy to be together at last.

It was a sad sound.

I was thinking of my mother. Missing my mother.

"How many do you say there are in that flock up there?" he said. He didn't take his eyes from the sky. The V formation was perfect except for a few extra on the end of the right leg of the V. If a couple of them would move over onto the end of the other leg of the V, it would be perfect.

"Not counting the last four on that long side, how many do you count?"

I figured if I counted one line and then doubled it, I'd have the answer. But as hard as I tried, I kept losing track. As the birds moved across the sky, they'd get ahead of my eyes and I'd be missing some or counting some twice. Each time, I'd have to start over at the lead goose. I tried using my arm in front of my eyes to block out the geese until I counted them. I tried using my hands as blinkers. I tried making a telescope out of my two fists. It didn't seem possible to count geese while they were flying.

"There's two hundred forty-four," Uncle Ronald said. "Two hundred forty-eight counting the four strays at the end."

We could hardly hear them now as they flew south, following the Gatineau River.

"They'll be over the Ottawa River in less than an hour," Uncle Ronald said.

I wondered if my mother would see them.

"It'll take those fancy policemen a lot longer than that to get home," Uncle Ronald chuckled. Then, back to the geese.

"Yessir, Lance," he said. "Two hundred and forty-eight geese. Imagine all those roasted up and set on a long, long table for Thanksgiving!"

Further up the road, where the creek ran along, Uncle Ronald nudged me and then out of his pocket he pulled the can of Odorama Tooth Powder. He got out of the rig and kneeled beside the creek, and snorting and whooping and gasping, did his mouth with the powder and the ice-cold creek water.

Back to the rig, he pulled out two short rods from the back, each with a line and a hook and a piece of red cloth for bait.

"Let's move up stream a ways," he said softly. "I might have frighted the fish a bit just now."

Might have.

In a quiet pool along a mossy log we floated our hooks with the red cloth and in the time it would take you to do a job on your teeth with Odorama Tooth Powder—a new thing—we had six sleek glistening little trout.

Uncle Ronald threaded a forked stick through the gills of each fish and laid them out on a cedar bough, like a fancy presentation in a store window.

"Let's make a visit, Lance," he said, and Lance knew just what to do.

He turned in without even being told to the house with the curved railings around the verandah and the apple trees. This horse was smart. He could probably write a book. Something like the dog, Beautiful Joe. Tell his life story. Story sort of the same. Going from a cruel master to a kind master.

The clouds were bruised blue, hanging low over the slanting black and gold field. Two crows called back and forward between two bare trees.

A pine grosbeak went *tew-tew!*

"Let's see if Cecelia Hickey likes these fish we brought," Uncle Ronald winked at me.

With the trout on the cedar bough cradled in one arm, Uncle Ronald knocked on the door and it opened while he was knocking. A man with a nose shaped like a sweet potato with a wart on the end of it the size of a big, ripe blueberry was already talking. He was glad to see us and would we come in for God's sake and stop standing out here in the chill.

There was a long black hair growing out of the wart on his nose.

He showed Uncle Ronald his teeth.

"Brand new," he said. "They just come in on the train last night from Toronto. Eaton's! The newest thing in false teeth. Sixty-day trial. If I don't like them after sixty days, I send them back!" He was saying he was glad to meet me and that he knew my mother and how long was I staying and a whole lot of other stuff when behind him came up his daughter Cecelia. Cecelia Hickey, the girl Uncle Ronald cleaned his teeth in the creek and brought the six trout on the cedar bough for.

"They're beauties. Thank you, Ronnie," she said and blushed and gave the fish to her father. "Put these in the cellar in the cool, Pa," she said, "while I take me two gentlemen callers into the parlor!"

Uncle Ronald nudged me. "She liked the fish," he whispered.

Mr. Hickey was still talking about his new teeth as he went out to the kitchen.

Cecelia had black hair, thin black eyebrows, black eyelashes, black pupils, white skin, white teeth, full red lips, red cheeks, a round head, a long back, a small nose, long fingers, a low voice.

"Wasn't it terrible about the policemen's nuts?" she said, laughing low in her throat and then blushing.

Then she told me she was glad I was there visiting because I'd be in the parlor with Ronnie and her and that would make it so her pa wouldn't have to come in and sit with them and spoil everything. I would be a kind of chaperone.

They'd just got the latest invention, a new talking and singing machine that you wound up with a crank—a gramophone—from Eaton's.

"Now that the train is so regular, you can get just about anything if you have the money—and Pa has the money—sent because of he was in the will of somebody dead back in Ireland—I don't know who it was and I don't care—and they've got electric streetcars now in Ottawa and I read in the paper two brothers in France invented a moving picture and ..."

Cecelia was putting on her favorite record as she talked: "The Bridal March from Lohengrin." She was pretty excited.

She and Ronnie played it over and over again until I got pretty sick of it.

She had three other records. One called "Just Because She Made Dem Goo-Goo Eyes!"—which was a dumb love song—and a funny talking story called "Casey and the Dude in the Street Car," and a song with a lot of whistling and laughing that made you laugh but you didn't know what you were laughing at called "The Laughing Fool."

They stopped playing "The Bridal March from Lohengrin" at last and let me play "The Laughing Fool" a few dozen times while they went and sat on the couch. While I was winding the crank of the gramophone again for about the fifth time, I looked up and saw Uncle Ronald kiss Cecelia on the nose and I saw her blush.

I guess the Odorama Tooth Powder was working pretty good.

We got invited for supper and Mr. Hickey all through supper was taking out his teeth and putting them back in and showing us where they pinched and where they pushed against his tongue. He could hardly talk with them in and when his mouth was full of potatoes it was even harder to understand him.

Cecelia said she didn't know how he was going to last the sixty-day free-trial period before he sent the teeth back, because this was only the second day and look at all the trouble he was having with them already.

They obviously didn't fit him because you could hear them clacking together when he was trying to eat and Cecelia was a little bit embarrassed and Uncle Ronnie looked up at me over his plate and said with his kind eyes that I'd better not laugh.

It was hard to eat while Mr. Hickey was doing those things with his teeth and while the hair growing out of the wart on his nose was springing and nodding around like a loose wire.

But none of us could help laughing when Mr. Hickey got into trouble with some tea that went down the wrong way and he coughed his teeth right out into the big bowl of boiled beets on the table.

He finally got the teeth out of the beet juice in the bowl and put them back in his mouth. The red beet juice was dripping off them and he looked a lot like a vampire that was just back from finishing a real nice snack someplace.

After supper Uncle Ronald and Cecelia and I decided

to take a quick ride back to Low to meet the train to see what the latest gossip was about the tax collectors.

On the way we stopped a couple of times to talk to some farmers. They told us some rumors and gossip about what happened to the tax collectors.

"They say they were scalded by water over at Flynn's," one farmer told us.

"They say that Mrs. O'Connor hit one of the lawyers over the head with a big stick," another farmer said.

Other rumors were that the bailiff was attacked by a vicious Thanksgiving turkey over at Nosey McCooey's and that at another place along the road the tax collectors were chased off by a wild gang of women with pitchforks.

Some said that some said that they heard that somebody warned that there would be bloodshed.

Somebody else saw somebody's kid wearing one of the policemen's funny hats.

Some said the farmers were getting guns and forming a gang.

Strangers would be sent home in wooden boxes, some said they said.

When we got there there was quite a crowd. Everybody had the same idea. We were wondering if there was anything in the paper about what happened. People were saying they'd be surprised if it got in the paper that fast but maybe there'd be something.

The rumors were going around about how the bailiffs and the lawyers and the policemen would soon have to take off back to Ottawa. Walking.

Walk all the way down the road in the mud back to Ottawa.

Some people said that they'd probably get somebody to rent them a wagon or two in Wakefield.

"That'll teach them to come up here and bother us!" some people were saying.

"But they haven't left yet," somebody said.

"Tomorrow's another day," somebody else said.

"Tell us something we don't know," somebody else said.

The train was right on time and not too many people got off.

The last person to get off was a woman with a bandage around her head. It was dark and she was partly in the lantern light of the platform around where the people were cutting the strings on the bundles of the *Ottawa Citizen* and *Journal*.

I moved closer. The woman looked familiar.

I moved closer.

It was my mother.

Her face was black with bruises and one eye was closed. One of her coat sleeves was empty.

"Oh, Mickey!" she said.

Uncle Ronald moved in around me and caught her as her knees buckled and she sank toward the platform.

13

Bark of the Pussywillow

SECOND CHANCE LANCE GOT US HOME IN A hurry after we dropped off Cecelia. He was nervous and wide-eyed, his eyes flashing in the lamps. He seemed to know there was violence around. Violence and pain. There was cruelty in the air. Second Chance Lance knew all about cruelty.

We brought my mother into the house and the O'Malley girls took over.

"Get Willy Willis at once!" they both said. Uncle Ronald touched my arm.

"We're going to get Willy Willis. You have to come and open the gates. It'll be faster. The sooner we get him here the better."

I looked into my mother's broken face.

She nodded painfully and we left. As I shut the door I watched the O'Malley girls moving around the kitchen, making my mother comfortable. They were grim and serious. Their faces were tight.

Lance pointed his head and after only a few steps he was into a speeding trot that made the spokes of our wheels whirr in the night. At the first gate we slowed to a walk and I jumped off and ran ahead and lifted the latch, opened the gate and hopped back on while the rig was moving.

Same with the second gate.

Not too far past Cecelia Hickey's (Uncle Ronald

only once looked up at her window and not for long) we swung to the right down a road I never noticed before, a narrow twisting lane through a thick stand of white pine, tall and straight and ghostly as we drove. It got darker and darker the deeper we moved until I wondered how Lance even stayed on the road.

"He has more than eyes," Uncle Ronald said. "He has an extra sense."

Some of the soft needles of the white pine trees along the road touched my coat as we whooshed by.

Soon, off in the trees there was a light showing and Lance headed in. The light was a lantern flickering in the stomach of a large statue of St. Joseph, his head tilted to one side and his hands out. Behind the statue was a tiny log cabin. It had a door and a small square window on the front and on one side another small square window showing a yellow warm glow.

The door squeaked open before we knocked. A little man with burning eyes and black teeth and a voice like burnt toast spoke to us.

"God bless you, Ronald. Who's the boy?"

"My sister's lad."

"What's happened? What brings you here?"

"My sister. She's been beaten."

"Where is she?"

"Over home."

"You'll take me." The little man turned and went into his cabin, the door closing squeaking shut.

"Who is he?" I whispered to Uncle Ronald.

"Faith healer," Uncle Ronald said. "And doctor."

There was a small water pump beside the statue of St. Joseph and hanging on a hook right next to the lantern in the stomach was a small pail. I filled the pail and gave Lance a drink. He thanked me by making a low, friendly sound deep in his throat. The cabin door opened and Willy Willis, faith healer and doctor, stood for a second in the light. He was checking the pockets of his short coat and feeling a big sack that he carried to see if he had everything he needed. He was very bow-legged and you could see a lot of the light that came from his cabin through the large opening between his legs.

Standing beside Uncle Ronald he looked like a little monkey.

Lance pulled us home like the wind.

The O'Malley girls had five kettles boiling on the stove.

They were bathing my mother's eyes with the whites of eggs.

Willy Willis got out a little bottle of holy water and sprinkled it around the room and crossed himself and blessed the room and my mother, and the O'Malley girls crossed themselves and we all knelt down and said some prayers that Willy Willis chanted real quick.

"Now," said Willy, "let's get on with the other part."

"That'd be just fine with me," my mother said through her swollen lips.

Willy Willis started pulling cures out of his sack and placing them on the oil-clothed kitchen table.

Each medicine was in a different shape. Some were little boxes of powder, some were twisted-looking roots, some were bark, some were big ugly dry leaves, some were little bottles of colored liquid, some were pieces of cloth soaked in something, some were seeds, some were oil, some were fat mixed with gum or wax.

Each time he placed a medicine on the table he blessed it with a tiny prayer and then said what each was to be used for.

The O'Malley girls nodded together each time, memorizing everything Willy Willis said, pressing their lips together, repeating after Willy Willis, making sure they memorized everything exactly right, pointing each time, each pointing with a short, tough, red finger.

"Spruce gum and lamb fat salve for infections..." Willy Willis said and hit the little glass jar hard onto the table, his burnt-toast voice rasping.

"Spruce gum and lamb fat salve for infections..." the O'Malley girls chanted after him, pointing close to the little, thick jar.

"Blessed be the Father, the Son and the Holy Ghost," Willy Willis muttered each time.

"Poppy tea for sleep," Willie Willis rasped and hammered his knuckles into the table where he placed the crushed-up dried leaves for the poppy tea.

The O'Malley girls repeated and pointed and waited for the next one.

"Cow lily pounded into a mash for swollen limbs and a solution for bathing..."

Blessed be the Father, the Son...

Repeat.

Hit the table.

Point.

"Horseradish root and a water solution to promote appetite..."

"Lambkill for swellings..."

"Skunk Cabbage—a piece of the root pressed against the gum to relieve toothache..."

"Bark of the pussywillow boiled to a thick paste— a poultice for bruises..."

"Holy Mary Mother of God..."

"Juniper gum for cuts and sprains..."

"Balsam sap for abrasions..."

"Cedar oil for swollen joints..."

"Parts of sumac tree steeped in blackberry juice for earache..."

By the time they were finished, the table looked like an apothecary's window display.

The O'Malley girls pushed a big copper tub out into the middle of the kitchen floor and began filling it with hot water from the kettles on the stove.

They began undressing my mother.

"Why didn't you run away?" Willy Willis asked my mother, sticking his face right in hers.

"I did," my mother said.

"Well?" said Willy.

"I went back," my mother said.

"Why?" Willy said.

"I remembered there was some money hidden in another place that slipped my mind."

"What happened?" Willy Willis asked. His voice was so raspy you wanted to clear your own throat while he was talking.

"You're very inquisitive, aren't you, Willy Willis?" my mother said, defiant, sticking her battered face up to his. "Maybe even a bit nosey!"

"Never mind that, my girl," Willy wheezed. "What happened?" After a bit my mother answered.

"I went in the house and he came right in after me. He said a friend of his, a porter at the Union Depot, saw me put Mickey on the train. He said if I followed, he'd come up and get us. Then he beat me."

"When you went back for the money, did you think to give him one more chance at the same time?" Willy asked, gentle as he could.

My mother looked away from Willy Willis' face but said nothing. The answer was a silent yes.

There was a long pause.

"Take me home," Willy said to Uncle Ronald.

14

Staked to a Manure Pile

WHILE WE TOOK WILLY WILLIS BACK HE TOLD
us all about how years ago he visited the famous
Brother Andre down at Cote-des Neiges under the
western slope of Mont Royal, Montreal's highest
mountain. Brother Andre was the doorman at the
College of Notre Dame over there and although he was
only a little, unimportant doorman and a messenger
and a barber and a handyman and did all the odd jobs
at this school for future priests, like doing the boys'
laundry and fixing shoes and sweeping the floor and all
that, he was also famous for curing the sick. He used
oil from the lamp burning in front of St. Joseph's statue in the college chapel. He rubbed the oil on the sick
who visited him.

And they got better. If they were crippled, they
could walk. If they were blind, they could see.

Brother Andre, even though he was only a doorman
at a school, was famous all over Canada for his cures and
his St. Joseph's oil. Joseph was Jesus' dad and was the
saint that all working, laboring poor people prayed to
when they were sick or hurt. All the ordinary people.

And Brother Andre gave Willy Willis a little bottle
of this magic St. Joseph's oil that time, that winter,
when Willy went all the way down to the west slope of
Mont Royal, Montreal's highest mountain, in the bit-
ter winter weather to visit Brother Andre. And Willy

brought the oil back to Low there to his little cabin. He didn't have much. He only used it sometimes. He had powers of his own.

He told us all this on the way home. He was pretty excited about it.

"And I'll use it on your mother tomorrow if she's worse," he said, as he climbed down from the rig. "St. Joseph would say she qualifies as a laboring person. She's laboring trying to make a silk purse out of a pig's arse!"

We let him off in front of the statue.

There was a bit of wind as he passed his light in the belly of the statue of St. Joseph outside his cabin and the flicker of the flame made Willy's shadow huge across his cabin and then small again. His legs made an "O" and then he was gone.

I asked Uncle Ronald what he meant.

"There's an old saying," Uncle Ronald explained as Lance came round and we left Willy's yard. "You can't make a silk purse out of a sow's ear. Willy changed it a bit. Your mother has tried for a long time to change your father from a mean man into a decent man—but Willy says it's hopeless. He says you might as well try to make a silk purse out of the south end of a pig," Uncle Ronald spoke in his soft, deep voice.

We were quiet all the way home. I was thinking it all over. Brother Andre and the mountain and Willy Willis and St. Joseph and the lamp oil and my mother and my father and a silk purse and a pig and the other end of a pig.

It made me smile and then I was ashamed of smiling, there in the dark, Lance and Uncle Ronald and I, whirring along in the dark.

When the warm yellow light from the farmhouse came round the turn, Lance did a throaty rumble.

At the stable Uncle Ronald undid the traces from the whippletree and eased Lance from between the shafts of the rig. He slung the leather traces over Lance's back gently. The traces, when they were in the air, frightened me, and when the metal hames clinked, Uncle Ronald noticed me raise my arm and pull back and turn my head away.

A look of great pity came over his face that I could see in the light of the stable lantern.

"Does your father beat you, too?"

I nodded, ashamed.

"Don't be ashamed," said Uncle Ronald.

He gave me Lance's reins, up short.

"You lead him into the stable. Just pull gently but confidently. He'll follow you."

I looked up into Lance's face. For a small horse he seemed pretty big from where I was. He was looking down his nose at me. His eyes were big and soft. He blinked them once.

"Well?" Second Chance's eyes said to me. "What kind of a person are you?"

I watched carefully while Uncle Ronald unbuckled Lance's bellyband and took off his harness and hung it up and rubbed Lance's back and neck where the collar and the bellyband had been. I paid close attention how the collar came off, how the breeching was unbuckled, how the reins unclipped from the bit, how the throat latch undid the bridle. How the steel bit came out of Lance's mouth across his teeth. How he seemed to enjoy it being gone. How he licked and chomped his teeth. He reminded me of Mr. Hickey trying to eat his supper.

We checked Lance's water, threw down some hay, rubbed Lance's nose, said goodbye to Lance, blew out Lance's lamps, locked the door quiet to Lance's stable.

Before we went into the house, Uncle Ronald told me something.

"When your father was your age," he said, "his father used to tie him to a stake on the manure pile and whip him with his horse whip. That's the way your father was brought up. I know. I was hiding once. I saw."

Inside, the kitchen was a mess. Water all over the floor, herbs and medicines and jars and powders and gum all over the table, soap on the stove. Rags and towels and clothes and bandages thrown around.

"They're upstairs," Ronald said, and we went up.

The O'Malley girls were standing on each side of my mother with their arms folded and smiling.

My mother was sitting up in bed surrounded by pillows and quilts. There were pots and bottles and dishes and vials and compresses on the two tables beside the bed. Four coal-oil lamps burned. The room was cheerful and bright and clean and smelled of flowers and starch and soap and mint and rhubarb and whiskey.

"We added some of our own cures," said the O'Malley girls. "That Willy Willis, he knows a lot, but he doesn't know everything! He doesn't know much about whiskey!"

After some talking, some laughing, some fussing, they blew out three of the lamps and left me alone with my mother.

She snuggled down into her luscious bed.

I had planned what I was going to say.

But I got it wrong.

"You can't make a pig's purse out of a silk south end," I said, knowing I had it all wrong.

My mother looked blank for a bit and then burst out laughing.

"Where did you get that, my darling boy?" she said.

"Willy Willis," I said. "But I think I said it wrong."

"That's all right, my boy, my boy, that's all right..." Then she cried some. And laughed again. "Oh, Mickey, what's to become of us?"

We hugged for a while until I noticed I was breathing in a horrible smell.

"It must be the skunk cabbage," my mother said when she saw my nose wrinkled up. "Don't worry, we'll get out of this. But we'll have to prepare. We'll have to get ready for him. Because he's comin'. As sure as the winter follows fall, he'll be here."

At home, in Ottawa, when we were sad and I couldn't get to sleep, my mother used to talk about picking berries and that way I'd get drowsy and...

"Tell about the berries," she said. "You remember how."

I did remember. I knew it all off by heart.

"The first berries are in the spring," I started. "The strawberries. They grow near the ground and they're shy and they hide behind their leaves and they're shaped like a tiny raccoon's nose and you pick them and put them in your mouth one at a time and they're so sweet and wild they surprise your mouth and you know you'll never forget the taste. Then comes, a few weeks later, the raspberries and they grow high off the ground and you tie a pail to your waist and tickle the berries off the vine with both hands so the berries go ping into your empty pail and be careful, watch the thorns, move slow through the canes so the thorns don't grab you. Then your pail is filling up and there's no more ping just a little plop each time and the sun is in each berry and the pail gets hotter and hotter from the sun-filled berries so that you can feel the heat on your face if you stick your head into the pail and the smell of the berries in there might make you faint..."

I was ready to tell the rest. Thimbleberry, blackberry, blueberry, gooseberry...then into the chokecherries and the plums and the black currants but she didn't need any more. She was peaceful asleep.

I breathed out her lamp and pulled her door soft shut.

15

A Dry Bed

EVEN STEVEN WAS OVER BRIGHT AND EARLY. Uncle Ronald was finished growling into his icy basin of water and going *"Woop! Woop! Woop!"* and cutting the kindling and banging the stove and showing the kettle who was boss.

Then, the rooster.

And me with the best feeling in the world: a dry bed!

And then the sound of Even Steven, excited, telling what he knew.

I went up and looked in my mother's room. She was sleeping as calm and quiet and safe as a spoiled cat. I went back down to the kitchen.

Yesterday, Even Steven did something he couldn't wait to tell us about.

"You shoulda seen me yesterday, Ronald and Mickey! I took the wagon up the road and picked up two of the McCooeys. I picked up Whistle McCooey and Mouthwash McCooey. Whistle has an old deer gun there with no bolt in it and I had along that rusty old Napoleon one-ball musket I have with the bayonet attached. I had that and we whittled up a board to look like the shape of a double-barrel shotgun for Mouthwash McCooey to hold and we drove by Brooks' Hotel in the wagon and the police sittin' right there on the verandah after their lunch gettin' ready to go back out harassin' innocent citizens..."

Uncle Ronald was getting the toast and the porridge onto the table while he listened. He had on a little smile while Even Steven was telling his story.

"Would the O'Malley girls be coming down to breakfast? Maybe they'd like to hear this..." Even Steven said, hope in his voice.

"No, they won't," said Ronald, mysterious. "They were up pretty late last night, working on a bit of a project..."

"A project? What kind of a project?"

"Oh, I wouldn't know," said Uncle Ronald. "Mickey and I, we were asleep, weren't we, Mickey?" Even Steven searched my face but I showed him nothing. Even Steven wanted to know everything and Uncle Ronald loved to keep him in the dark. Tell him nothing. Just to tease him a bit.

"People are all sayin' that it was them after all who took the nuts from the policemen's wagons..." Even Steven said, his face full of hope.

"Oh, we wouldn't know anything about that, now. The O'Malley girls, they don't say much, do they, Mickey?"

I shook my head.

"It's a mystery," said Even Steven, his eyes narrow. Then he brightened up. "Well, anyway," he took up his yarn again, "me and the two McCooeys— Mouthwash and Whistle—sail right past their verandah, right past their noses in our wagon with our guns pointing toward the sky. You shoulda seen them soldiers gawkin' at us! And Mouthwash, cursin' and swearing better 'n I've ever heard him. He uttered some swearin' there Ronald I swear I've never in my life heard before.

90 ∽

He's the best. And I've worked in the shanties in the bush and don't you think I haven't heard more than my share of professional, top-of-the-line cursin'! And all the while there's Whistle McCooey, sittin' there with his gun, whistlin' a jig of some kind, whistlin' away, and Mouthwash cursin' away and the policemen on the verandah gawkin'. Oh, it was grand, Ronald and young Mickey. You shoulda been there for it!"

"We heard some rumors about guns, didn't we, Mickey, yesterday evening..."

"The only trouble with it was we couldn't get Mouthwash to face the policemen on the verandah as we drove by. He was swearin' real good, like I said, but he would only face straight ahead the whole time. We drove past more than a few times but he'd only face straight ahead, he wouldn't look at the police, so it lost a little bit of impact, you might say, him swearing straight ahead like that each time. But Whistle—that was a different thing altogether! Whistle whistled that jig right at them police, them paid assassins, each time we passed, right at them, bold as you please! Oh, it was grand! I wish you coulda been there, the two of ya!

"And another thing," Even Steven went on. "They say that there's a reporter got off the train last night at Brennan's Hill and he's been sending reports by telegraph and courier down to Ottawa!"

"Might be something in the papers tonight, then," Uncle Ronald said.

"Then we'll find out everything that's been goin' on!" Even Steven said.

"You think the paper will know more than we ourselves know, Steven?" Uncle Ronald asked.

"Sure enough! The papers, they know it all eventually!"

You could tell Uncle Ronald didn't believe this for a minute but he didn't say so. He was not the type to argue.

"Maybe," he said, giving me a look, "they'll tell us who removed the nuts from the policemen's wagons."

"Maybe they will," said Even Steven.

"Maybe they'll say *you* did it," said Uncle Ronald to Even Steven.

"Maybe they will," said Even Steven, blushing. You could tell he would love to get his name in the paper. He had the look of a lad who would love to be a little bit famous for a while, maybe.

"Maybe you're the one murdered that Bailiff Flatters some while back," said Uncle Ronald, teasing.

Even Steven started wiggling in his chair and getting a deeper color and half laughing and half frowning.

He had the look of a lad who'd never ever murder a bailiff but wouldn't mind if people *said* that he did.

Behind Even Steven I saw my mother slip past the stairs and disappear into the parlor.

Uncle Ronald was poaching an egg in a small pan while Even Steven was acting like he was getting ready to leave. Each time he'd be leaving for sure, he wouldn't leave.

It was like watching waves pretend to leave a sandy shore and then come right back again. He kept remembering new pieces of gossip, new rumors.

I slipped out into the parlor and sat with my mother.

"We'll be ready for him when he comes," she whispered. It was what she was saying before she went to sleep the night before. It was almost as though she'd been saying it all night long and was still saying it this morning.

"I want you to steal a sharp meat-cutting knife from the kitchen when the O'Malley girls and Ronnie aren't looking. Steal it and bring it up to my bedroom, hide it under the mattress. And don't breathe a word!"

I went back into the kitchen.

Uncle Ronald was holding Even Steven gentle but strong by the elbow and helping him out the door. He was still talking after the door was shut.

My mother came in and sat down.

We hugged her and kissed her and said she looked a lot better, which was a lie.

"I know that's not true," she said. "I don't look better, I look worse, but I'll tell you something...I FEEL a whole lot better, I really do. Coming back up to Low was the right thing, the smart thing to do. And I'll tell you something else. I'll never go near that man again, so help me God!"

Then she ate her poached egg and asked for a couple more.

With thick toast, if you please.

And Uncle Ronald went back to showing the stove who was boss.

When he went out to do the chores I stole a long sharp knife out of the drawer and took it upstairs and hid it under my mother's mattress.

After the chores, Uncle Ronald gave me a lesson in harnessing Second Chance Lance and hitching him up to the rig.

First we put on Lance's collar. It made me laugh the way Lance pointed his head straight out so that it would be easy to slip the collar over his ears and onto his shoulders. He reminded me of a little kid putting up his arms so his mom could pull his sweater on for him.

Then Uncle Ronald smoothed Lance's back with a brush and threw the back pad over on him and moved it around a bit until it was comfortable. Then he cinched the bellyband tight. Uncle Ronald pulled the straps of the bellyband through the buckle quite hard—hard enough to make Lance step sideways to catch his balance.

Then the long leather traces got clipped to the metal hames on the collar.

Next was the leather breech straps around his rump which got hooked to the bellyband to keep the rig from running up on him from behind when he put on the brakes.

Then the crupper under his tail.

And last, the bridle around his head and the bit in his mouth.

He took the bit in his mouth like he didn't like the taste of the cold metal as he worked his tongue around it and while it thwocked against his teeth.

Then the reins got clipped onto the bit and the traces draped over his back.

Then I got to walk him over to the wagon. Gee. Haw.

Gee meant go to the right.

Haw meant go to the left.

Uncle Ronald backed Lance between the shafts of the rig and clipped the traces to the whippletree.

Ready to go.

But we didn't go anywhere.

"Now," Uncle Ronald looked at me, "to unhitch him we do the same only in reverse. Can you remember the order? It's easier to unhitch than to hitch. You tell me the steps and we'll see if you have it right."

"Right now?" I said.

"Right now," he said.

"Unclip the traces from the whippletree and lead Lance out from between the shafts," I said, hardly believing my own ears.

Uncle Ronald looked at me with deep affection in his face.

I got through the whole process with only a couple of mistakes.

We hung all the harness up on the proper pegs in the stable and patted Lance goodbye and shut the door.

"Now," said Uncle Ronald, "let's go in and you hitch him up this time!"

We went back in.

I took the collar down from the peg and held it up as high as I could. Uncle Ronald supported it a little higher for me and we waited to see if Lance would point his head for me.

See if he would accept me.

He looked at first a little impatient. "Didn't we just go through all this?" Lance's face seemed to say.

Then he pointed his head.

With Uncle Ronald's help, I ran the collar up over his head and onto his shoulders.

"You're on your way," Uncle Ronald said confidentially to me, as though he didn't want to embarrass

Lance. "He's your friend. He's going to let you harness him."

Uncle Ronald had to help me with tightening the bellyband, but I did most of the rest of it pretty well by myself.

All those belts and buckles.

I never thought I would ever like the feel of belts and buckles.

When we were back hitched to the rig again, Lance was anxious to go this time. Uncle Ronald noticed a trace carrier was coming loose, and also some stitches on the breeching were coming undone, so he decided we'd take a trip over to Even Steven's place. Steven had a new outfit called the Farmer's Friend, a riveter that he got out of Eaton's catalogue a while back. You could repair harness with rivets instead of stitching.

On our way over to Even Steven's we came to an open, rocky clearing near the brow of a small hill.

As sudden as a clap of thunder, up over the hill from the other side a V of barking geese came roaring, flying low, gabbling and burbling and arguing.

They were so low you could hear their wings plowing the air.

Lance pulled up.

"How many this time?" Uncle Ronald yelled out to me, even though I was sitting right beside him.

"How do you count them?" I called out, feeling I could reach up and pull one down by the feet.

"The way you learned to harness Lance!" Uncle Ronald shouted, laughing.

The way I learned to harness Lance.

Of course!

Backwards! From the back!

I jumped from the rig and started counting one arm of the V from the end.

How easy. The geese seemed motionless in the sky.

There were sixty-five geese counting the leader.

The other arm had one extra straggler.

"One hundred and thirty!" I shouted. "One hundred and thirty!"

"Exactly," said Ronald, more quiet now, and put his arm out to help me back on the rig and patted my shoulder and squeezed the back of my neck and pushed my hat down over my eyes and ruffled my hair.

"We'll pick up the Farmer's Friend at Stevens' and then head right into town to the station—see what's the latest," said Uncle Ronald, partly to Second Chance Lance, partly to me.

16

The O'Malley Girls Is One

Rumors were flying around the station.

Even Steven and the two McCooeys had followed the police around in the afternoon after Father Foley found some new nuts for their wagons. The rules were if the people didn't have the money to pay the taxes that they owed, the police could take their stuff, their furniture, their animals, their tools. But they had to leave the people with two of everything. Two pigs, two horses, two cows, two chairs, two pitchforks, like that. Like in Noah's ark. They had a list of everybody and how much they owed. But they didn't get very far because people were hiding stuff. At one place somebody poured a full chamber pot on them. At another place they buttered the front steps and everybody fell down. At another place they chained the hay rake to the house and blocked the door. At another they put a team of horses in the kitchen ...

The freight man was off the train before it even got stopped. He ran up and down the platform waving the *Evening Journal* and the *Daily Citizen*.

"It's all in the papers!" he was roaring to everybody. "It's all in the papers! Front page. We're on the front page. Everybody. It's all there!"

The bundles of papers tumbled out onto the platform and hardly any attention was paid to the regular baggage. The twine on the bundles was cut and the papers passed around while the cars of the train were still shuddering from the stop.

THEIR BLOOD UP!

was one big headline.

"Our blood is up!" shouted one farmer, his finger on the words, his paper raised high.

LOW MEN SAY THEY WILL FIGHT

BEFORE THEY WILL GIVE IN!

the smaller headline said.

"Yes, they will!" cheered another farmer, waving his hat in the air.

"You mean, 'Yes, WE will," shouted his friend and slapped him on the back so hard he fell against the side of the station.

"I mean, 'WE will,'" cheered the first one, slamming his hat back on his head so hard he had to take a step back.

MOB GATHERING

OFFICERS THREATENED

a smaller heading announced.

"A mob is gathering!" shouted Turnaround McCooey, running from group to group, turning and spinning with excitement.

"*We* are the mob, ya damn fool, ya!" somebody shouted and everybody laughed and cheered.

"Ya can't believe everything ya read in the papers!" somebody else shouted.

"WRONG!" another one said. "Everything you see in the papers is the honest to God TRUTH!" And everybody clapped and agreed.

THE POSSE TOO SMALL

TO COPE WITH THE MOB

a headline on another page said.

Nobody was paying any attention to the train or who was getting off.

People stood under the lamps in little groups.

One person would read some out loud then pass the paper to the next one to have a turn.

At the end of the platform a woman read a part about her neighbor who gave a big speech about Ireland to a tax collector—it was quite a speech, the paper said—and when the woman got to that part she burst out laughing and raised her fist in the air and cheered. Then she handed her spectacles and the paper on to the next person and that person read some more out loud.

Another group was reading about the police and a bailiff approaching the door of "delinquent ratepayer" John O'Rorke.

John O'Rorke himself was reading it out loud. Then he stopped.

"This is about *me*, for Gawd's sake!" he said. "This is about me!"

"Read it, John, read it in your best voice, like you've never read anything before. Give us your best, John!" people were pleading.

The train was leaving but nobody even noticed.

John O'Rorke cleared his throat and read in his best, serious voice, with a little bit of an accent, like an English actor on a stage:

The first of the delinquent ratepayers on the list was John O'Rorke. Arriving at the O'Rorke house, Constable Genest and a bailiff approached the door, which was opened by a daughter of Mr. O'Rorke.

"Is Mr. John O'Rorke at home?" asked Constable Genest.
"He's dead," replied the daughter.
"Well, who is in charge of this place?" asked the constable.
"I am. What do you want?" was the reply.

"His taxes are not paid, and I have come to collect them,"
said Constable Genest, as he advanced to walk into the house,
followed by Sergeant Patry and Mr. Major. "Ye's'll not git in
here," was the reply of the young woman in the doorway,
defiant. "I'll throw boiling water on ye if ye come any fur-
ther," and suiting her action to her word she rushed toward
the center of the house where a pot of water was boiling on a
cooking stove...

"Oh, Gawd help me I can't go on..." said O'Rorke and fell down on the platform holding his sides.

"We didn't know you were dead, John! When was the wake? Did we miss it altogether?" somebody asked and a wave of enjoyment went up and down the platform.

My mother and I and Uncle Ronald and Even Steven were reading our paper by the light of the dark-lamp on Lance's rig.

"Look here," said Steven, his eyes glowing. "Here's the part about the 'rebels' sabotaging the policemen's rigs. The paper calls us 'rebels'!"

"Us?" my mother said, turning to Steven. "Are you one of the 'rebels' who 'sabotaged' the policemen's rigs?"

"Well, no, I guess I wasn't, but I think I know who did!"

"Steven challenged the police, though, didn't you, Steven?" Uncle Ronald said. "Didn't you go by with the two McCooeys and the rusty guns in the wagon by Brooks' verandah while the police were sittin' out there after their lunch, pickin' their teeth?"

"I did that. That's for sure!" said Steven.

"Is that in the paper?" my mother said.

"Yes, it's right here." Uncle Ronald pointed to the paragraphs using the words "dangerous rebels" and "menacing" and "armed to the teeth," "threats of attack" and "apprehension of bloodshed."

"Do you believe what you read in the newspapers, Steven?" said my mother, who was feeling even better after being out in the fresh air. She felt good enough to want to tease Steven.

"The papers, they tell what they saw," said Steven, a serious look on his face.

"You and the two McCooeys, is this what the paper's referring to as 'dangerous, menacing rebels'? And it says here, 'hundreds who would just as soon fight as eat'?"

"I'll fight fer me rights," said Steven, sticking out his chin.

"You and the two McCooeys. That's three, not hundreds!"

"There's the O'Malley girls," said Uncle Ronald.

"Then that's five," said my mother.

"No, that's four," said one of the farmers who was listening in. "You see, the O'Malley girls is just ONE!" While the eavesdropping farmer was cackling away at his own joke, Uncle Ronald got serious for a minute.

He read from a small added part to the story at the bottom of the back page.

"What does that mean?" said Steven, looking a little uneasy.

"It means they're comin' back," said Uncle Ronald. "Bigger and better next time."

"Well, we'll be ready for them," said Steven, but not very loud.

While they were talking back and forward like this about what was in the paper, what they were saying faded further and further away until I couldn't hear them any more.

There was one thing and one thing only taking up all my attention right now.

And that was I thought I saw a familiar shape duck around behind the end of the station a minute before.

The shape was the shape of my father.

17

Burn Like Ice

THE NEXT MORNING I WOKE UP IN A PISSED-IN bed.

There was nobody around. I missed the rooster, I missed Uncle Ronald's morning racket. My mother wasn't in her room, the O'Malley girls were gone, breakfast was over, the dishes were done.

I filled a basin of warm warm water from the kettle on the stove and sponged myself down with a cloth.

I got dressed.

I carried the mattress out to the barn and emptied it out into the manger. The cows wouldn't know the difference. I rinsed out the mattress bag in the drinking trough and hung it up on two hooks on a beam to dry.

On my way back to the house I looked in on Second Chance Lance.

He was gone.

I was filled with dread.

I hadn't told anybody about what I'd seen at the station the night before.

I had gone to bed, silent, worrying about it. Maybe it wasn't him at all. And then again, maybe it was.

I went to sleep with horrible thoughts.

I dreamt.

Even Steven was at my window with one of the McCooey's heads on instead of his own head. Mr.

Hickey was chewing off my leg with his new Eaton's catalogue teeth. My mother flew over, large and larger until her bruises turned into the color of the bruised November sky. Willy Willis was screaming at the statue of St. Joseph until the fire in its belly reached out for him. Second Chance Lance was dead in a little dog basket, his ears cut off.

And in my dreams my father was nowhere, but he was everywhere. In everything, behind everything, under everything.

This morning, the house was silent. Creaked a bit. Then, only the clock in the parlor, ticking and tocking.

And the last house fly of the year, caught between the windows, trying every now and then to drill his way through the glass.

I put a stick of wood in the fire and picked up two pails and headed out to get some water (O'Malley girls' rule of the house, if you use water, go and get some more).

I picked my way down the clay path across the potato field, keeping my pails silent.

On a bare ironwood tree by the edge of the potato field a hairy woodpecker clutched and said *PIK!* and then did the noise of a green stick drawn along a picket fence.

One thousand one hundred million years ago, before the beginning of life, those Gatineau hills were formed.

Four hundred million years ago a great sea floated there.

Seventy-five million years ago the dinosaurs ran there.

Ten thousand years ago, another sea, the Champlain sea, dumped all that clay there.

Nine thousand years ago, human hunters from north and south met there, amazed.

One hundred years ago, I walked down that same clay to get two pails of water. I snapped the first pail on the hook and watched the pail ride down and hit the water. I watched it sink and fill.

I wound the full pail up and sent the second down.

While I cranked up the second pail I thought I saw my father again, standing at the bottom of the cliff by the well, looking up at me, waving, friendly.

I shut my eyes and when I opened them, he was gone.

I lifted the two pails and started back.

Ahead of me, limping along the cold clay path, was a curled-up maple leaf, struggling along like an old, crippled spider.

The sun was out, bright, and the breeze was icy.

My eyes filled.

The hot tears on my cheeks burned like ice.

All of a sudden, blind, I tripped and went down on my knees, dumping the pails.

The ancient clay became the sky, the bright sun turned and spun.

Then it was Uncle Ronald lifting me up and holding onto me, saying what's wrong, saying it's all right now, it's all right now...

Back in the house he said it didn't matter if I wet the bed, that he used to wet the bed and what did it matter, it's only straw or hay or clover or thistles or what and the cows will eat it, anyway, in fact they like it better that way and maybe we should all get together and piss in our beds regularly—the O'Malley girls, your mother, Even Steven and everybody—and haven't you noticed your friend Second Chance Lance, he doesn't care where he lets go, day or night...

And he went on like this to cheer me up until he made me laugh and then told me that this was the day, Saturday, that a couple of our down-the-road neighbors picked up the O'Malley girls and went down to the general store and they took your mother with them and she's not only feeling better but she's even lookin' better...and everything's going to be all right...

I didn't tell him what I thought I saw.

That afternoon (after Uncle Ronald helped me fill my mattress bag with fresh straw, hay and clover—no thistles for sure this time) my mother and the O'Malley girls came home and we all went over to the Hickeys' for a short visit.

Second Chance Lance liked it when the rig was full of people. There were five of us and I was squeezed in the back between my mother and one of the O'Malley girls.

Uncle Ronald was chanting a little jig under his breath...

The horse is in the stable
The pork is in the brine
The dinner's on the table
The washing's off the line...

Lance was speeding up on the turns, and when the O'Malley girls would squeal and say "Wheeee!" Lance would go even faster.

The hay is in the hay mow
The water's in the pail
The beans are in the pot now
Let it snow and hail ...

After a few fast curves, Lance slowed down on a straight stretch.

Up behind us came a running man. He was calling something to us. We heard it as he raced past us.

"Soldiers comin'," he cried out. "Soldiers comin'!"

"That's Twelve Toes McCooey!" Uncle Ronald told us. "He's spreading a rumor he heard. Somebody told him to run up and down the road and tell everybody. I wouldn't be at all surprised if he was right. You know, he can run almost as fast as Lance can!"

"That should be exciting," my mother said. "Soldiers. Soldiers to come and collect a few dollars in taxes? How much do you owe in taxes, Ronald, do you know?"

"I owe six dollars and thirty cents."

"Are ye goin' to pay it?"

"Sure, I'll pay it, if they fix the roads and build us a local school."

"What's the most somebody would owe?"

"Oh, about ten or twelve dollars or so," said Uncle Ronald.

"I have some money I can give to ya," my mother said, and I looked up at her. I knew where she got the money.

She drew me close and whispered, pressing her lips to my ear. "I got the knife. I sewed a sling for it on the inside of my left sleeve. I've got the knife there now. Can you feel it? All I have to do is have my right hand up my sleeve, and when he comes at me, I'll whip it out and stick him with it."

She was whispering in a normal whisper.

I could hardly believe what she was saying.

What she was saying, what she was whispering, filled me with fear.

Up ahead, a man came running toward us at top speed.

"Here comes Twelve Toes again!" said the O'Malley girls.

He passed by us so fast we couldn't hear what he said. We couldn't make it out.

"What was he saying?" I asked.

"Soldiers comin', I guess," said Uncle Ronald. "Same as before!"

Then Uncle Ronald went back to his song.

> *Keep the butter churning*
> *The sheep are in the pen*
> *The year is quickly turning*
> *And winter's here again.*
> *The wood is in the woodbox*
> *The fire's in the stove...*
> *I'll go and catch a woodcock*
> *And bring it to my love...*

We pulled into the Hickeys' yard and piled out of the rig.

No sooner did we get into Hickeys' and hang our hats and coats behind the stove so they'd get warm than Mr. Hickey started showing everybody the new teeth he got from Eaton's catalogue.

Then Cecelia showed us her cats: one that had a mustache; one that caught at least six birds a day and had a little graveyard corner in the granary where it kept all the bones, beaks and claws and feathers; and another cat that she said that Willy Willis examined and said it had a bad heart.

Then later we all peeled apples for applesauce and Cecelia showed us what her dead mother showed her, which was how to peel an apple and leave the peel in only one long single curly piece and then she cried a little bit about her mother.

And my mother and the O'Malley girls cried a little bit, too, but very quiet.

Then later in the afternoon people got drowsy and Cecelia's two dogs lay down under the table so relaxed you could hear their bones knock on the floor.

Then, in from the parlor came the sound of a fiddle.

I went in and there was Uncle Ronald by the window, the fiddle under his chin, his big fingers so delicate on the strings, the long notes sad.

When his love song was over he lowered his bow and plucked some single notes on the strings with his fingers while he looked out the window at Cecelia's gnarled, bare apple trees.

Then he turned to me and winked and started a fast pounding beat on the floor with the heel of his boot that echoed through the house, turning the house into a thunder box.

"I asked her to marry me!" Uncle Ronald said and then began to sing:

Smoke goes up the chimney,
We dance around the room.
Songs of love within me
Snow be comin' soon!

And then everybody woke up again and Cecelia played on the new gramophone "The Bridal March from Lohengrin" a couple of times and then Uncle Ronald told me to wind up the gramophone again and they played "The Bridal March from Lohengrin" again and again until my mother and the O'Malley girls were rolling their eyes and Mr. Hickey was back asleep on the sofa and his teeth were out on the floor and the cat with the bad heart was pushing them quiet out into the hallway, playing with his sixty-day teeth.

After a big snack of bread and butter and sweet blueberry jam and tea we went home and I helped Uncle Ronald split some firewood, each piece almost exactly the same size.

"This is a Christmas present for Cecelia. I'm giving her a perfect cord of this beautiful ash for firewood. The finest in the country. To keep her warm this winter."

It was almost dark but the perfect triangles of the pieces of white split ash in the even pile at the side of the shed still shone.

My mother was going to bed early. I carried her coal-oil lamp upstairs for her and tucked her in.

"You were awful quiet today, Mickey, me son. Are you troubled?"

I lied to her that I wasn't and that I was just thinking about everything and wondering what was going to happen.

"What's going to happen?" I asked her, looking into her beautiful face there in the moving flame of the lamp, her bruises fading.

"We're not goin' back to him. Not in this world, me son, you can be rest assured of that," she sighed.

Then I told her.

"I saw him," I said. "Twice. Once at the station last night. Once at the well this morning. He's here."

"Well, then," she said, her face flushing red. "Blow out the lamp and we'll wait for him."

After a long silence in the dark, my mother said these words—words spoken one hundred years ago— and I can hear them still, this day, spoken in her strong soft whisper.

"There are two kinds of fire, my son. The fire of love and the fire of hate. He has changed the flames of love I once burned for him into a scorching, searing hate!

"And he'll get what's comin' to him!"

18

Sit Down and Shut Up

WHAT TOMMY TWELVE TOES MCCOOEY RAN UP and down announcing was true. The papers the train brought said it all:

TROOPS FOR LOW!
DETACHMENT OF 43RD RIFLES
ORDERED FOR DUTY!
DELINQUENT SETTLERS
IN A THREATENING MOOD!
A CALL TO ARMS!
MILITIA TO WADE IN MUD THROUGH LOW!

The next morning, Sunday, in church, Father Foley gave a sermon telling the people to pay their taxes. It's what God would want his flock to do. Then he called a meeting for right after mass.

At the meeting, Even Steven surprised everybody. He got up on his feet and asked Father Foley, bold as you please, what God cared about taxes, wasn't He more interested in our souls?

Father Foley told him to sit down and shut up. Everybody laughed except Uncle Ronald. He turned to me and said, "Steven is going to do something great one of these times. Something people will be proud of!"

Around noon, when the meeting was about over, we heard the train whistle.

Everybody piled out and down to the station.

Sure enough, a special train, with an army on board!

The station was buzzing.

Rumors were flying.

The train supposedly took longer than the regular train because they had to stop and check each bridge for dynamite. There was no dynamite. Only rumors of dynamite.

The papers had said that the mob was growing and getting uglier and uglier.

Barnyard McCooey was going around saying to everybody he met, "*You* might be gettin' uglier and uglier, but I'm stayin' just the same!" And then he'd imitate a goat or a cow.

The train had two carloads of men and four carloads of horses. And another carload of supplies.

It was the best train yet!

People were happy, cheering, laughing, clapping, pointing, commenting, as the soldiers and horses unloaded.

The soldiers were handsome and smart in their uniforms. The horses were strong and sleek. The smell of the polished harness and the squeak of the soldiers' boots and the clank of the ammunition boxes and the thudding of the rifles on the platform!

Peek-a-boo McCooey was everywhere you looked.

Boys were playing soldier.

Kids were wrestling.

Older girls were tying ribbons, brushing each other's hair. Women were feeling the bales of tent canvas, admiring the cases of canned meat. Men were shaking hands with the soldiers, patting them, smelling the oiled rifles.

There were over a hundred soldiers.

And over fifty horses!

What a show!

The next day, Monday, the soldiers started a house-to-house search for delinquent taxpayers. They had a huge wagon to take away your belongings if you had no money.

The O'Malley girls put a plan into action.

The family of the first house took everything they owned and went off and hid back in the bush with all of it. Cattle, furniture, clothes, pets, everything. Mildred (or was it Edith?) stationed herself in the empty house, dressed completely in clothes made of sugar bags to show how poor she was.

When the officials opened the door she invited them in for hot water because she didn't have any tea and would they like to sit down except there wasn't any chairs and what can I do for ya?

Since there was nothing there they could take and since she told them that the family that used to live here were all gone back to Ireland, all they could do was ask her to sign a paper and when she said she couldn't read or write, they just gave up and left.

They didn't know that when they got to the next house up the road, the other O'Malley girl was there playing the same trick.

And while she was doing exactly the same business with them, the first O'Malley girl left the first house and cut through the back fields behind the trees and set herself up in the *third* house.

The officials were mad and confused after visiting about half a dozen houses where in each house exactly the same woman was in charge of the exact same thing—nothing!

Meanwhile, the soldiers marched up and down the muddy road.

In the evening we talked about it all and laughed about how the O'Malley girls fooled the officials and confused them so.

I thought I might tell Uncle Ronald the next morning about my mother's plans with the meat-cutting knife but I remembered my mother's warning not to breathe a word.

Before I went to bed I thought I might tell one of the O'Malley girls—or both of them—but how can you tell a secret to somebody when you're not sure who that somebody is?

In the kitchen, one of the O'Malley girls must have been reading my mind.

"Now, Mickey, I suppose you're wondering how you're ever goin' to be able to figure out how to tell us apart, me and me sister. Whether I'm Edith or Mildred or what. Or Mildred or Edith or who."

"Which one are you?" I looked into her brown eyes while I asked the words, while I wondered what difference it was going to make, anyway, whatever she told me.

"I'm Mildred, you see, Mickey. But telling you this won't do you a bit of good. You see, pet, you're no further ahead now, are you?"

"No, I guess not," I said. "Mildred."

"Because, as you are well aware, the next time you see me come in the room you still won't have any way of knowin' if I'm me or me sister Edith. And if it happens to be Edith you next see you won't know whether it's her or me!" She was smiling the whole while she was telling me this, laughing a bit, too.

"What do I do when I see you both together?"

"You must watch us very carefully, Mickey," she said, sudden solemn. "Because we're very different in one way and one way only."

"Which way is that? Please tell me. I have to know," I said.

"Better if you watch carefully, Mickey. In the meantime, I'll give you a little riddle to help you along. Here's your riddle:

WHEN I LOOK IN THE MIRROR
AND RAISE ONE HAND
I SEE MY SISTER.

Later, I watched both of the sisters together, working in the kitchen. They were talking about a big sharp meat-cutting knife that they couldn't seem to find anywhere no matter where they looked. I noticed that their clothes were exactly the same except for the aprons. Both aprons were sewn out of old sugar bags. You could still read the faded lettering that was almost washed out. The lettering was different. One apron said ATLANTIC SUGAR and the other one said RED-PATH SUGAR. The Redpath Sugar letters were in faded red and the Atlantic was in blue.

All I had to do now was find out whose was whose or which was which.

While I was reading the aprons the clock in the other room donged eight times and the O'Malley girls took off their aprons and knelt down, one hand on the kitchen table and said their prayers. I knelt down, too, but I wasn't praying. I was watching them to see if there was any difference between the way they said their prayers.

And I kept my eye on their aprons. The O'Malley girl on the left had put her apron on the back of a chair and the other O'Malley girl had laid hers down across the basin on the wooden washstand.

When they were finished their prayers, the O'Malley girl on the left picked up the apron that was across the washbasin and the O'Malley girl on the right ...

They'd switched aprons!

That night I put myself to sleep wondering what it was about the picture I had in my brain of the two O'Malley girls, kneeling, praying, one hand each on the kitchen table.

They were so the same.

Except for one thing.

But I couldn't see it.

And the little riddle.

The O'Malley girl looking in the mirror, one hand up. What does she see? Her sister?

A little riddle.

More like a big riddle it was to me then.

And then the morning, the wet, cold bed, the shame, the fear.

When was he coming?

Why didn't he come now, and get it over with?

19

Steven Hero

THE NEXT DAY, AT ONE OF FATHER FOLEY'S meetings, Even Steven became a hero. And he is still known in some parts—even after a hundred years has passed—he is still known as the man who alone, single-handedly, all by himself, with help from nobody, defeated an army and sent them home!

Here's what happened.

Father Foley was having one of his meetings. He'd just finished telling another farmer to sit down and shut his mouth. Nobody knew what to do. The bailiffs wanted money. The farmers had no money. The soldiers were here to frighten the money out of the farmers.

"You can't get blood out of a turnip," one farmer said for the hundredth time.

"And even if you, ahem, frighten, ahem, a turnip," said Ahem McCooey, "it still won't give you, ahem, any of its, ahem, blood because as, ahem, everybody, ahem, knows a turnip hasn't got any, ahem, blood in it!"

Uncle Ronald had been thinking about this problem ever since the first bailiff got locked in the cellar a couple of years before.

That night at the meeting he had an idea that he was sure would work. He also had a plan. He would give this good idea to Even Steven and let him present it. That way Steven could get the attention that he always wanted.

Uncle Ronald stood up and Father Foley gave him the floor.

"Father," said Uncle Ronald, "Steven and I and some of us have been discussing an idea that we had and we've decided that the best person among us to present the idea would be Steven so here he is, Father, with what we think is the solution to our problems!"

Even Steven got up but nobody would listen at first until Uncle Ronald got up and asked Father Foley if Steven could have a bit of attention and Father Foley told everybody to shut up and listen to Steven and they did.

It didn't take Steven long to present the idea.

He told the crowd that since Thanksgiving was coming up in a few days that it would be safe to say that the lawyers and the bailiffs and the officials and the soldiers would very likely like to be home for Thanksgiving dinner and they would probably be happy to be offered anything so they could go home.

"But we haven't GOT anything!" shouted about fifty farmers.

"Ah, yes," said Steven, "but we could all PROMISE to pay, don't you see! We could all sign a big affydavy sayin' that we PROMISE to pay and get Father Foley to witness it and bless it and everything else!"

You could tell right away that it was a good idea because everybody started talking about it and forgot about everything else they'd been talking and arguing about for the last year or so.

In no time at all Father Foley got the whole thing going and elected a council to take a list of everybody's name to the officials—a list of promises to pay.

And Even Steven got elected to the committee.

And in the early hours of the next morning, the tax collectors agreed and the army started packing to go home!

Steven was the hero.

The man who, with a single idea, sent home an army!

Hurrah for Steven!

20

And You Said You Loved Only Me

AROUND NOON THAT DAY MY MOTHER WAS helping me harness Second Chance Lance. I told her all about how Lance got his name and how Uncle Ronald saved him and gave him a new life just like the dog in the book she gave me, *Beautiful Joe*.

"Except the book is hard to read," I said, "because the dog tells the story and you keep thinking how can a dog write a book!"

My mother had a nice look on her face and said, "It's only a book."

I was showing off how I knew how to harness Lance by myself and I told her how Uncle Ronald had showed me by first *un*harnessing Lance.

And that reminded me of how I learned to count geese in the air by counting from the back of the V instead of the front.

"That Ronnie," she said. "He's a smart good one, he is. You could do worse modeling yourself after that man and I'm not saying that just because he's me brother."

My mother knew how to harness a horse but she'd forgotten a lot of it.

When we got to tightening the bellyband, we both pulled as hard as we could but we knew it wasn't tight enough. The buckle had to be cinched up one more hole to be properly in place.

We were planning to go out for a little ride, just the two of us. I was going to try to talk her out of her plan to use the knife to stick in my father.

We hitched Second Chance Lance to the rig and left him there and then started walking back to the house to get Uncle Ronald to come and tighten Lance's belly-band properly for us.

As we rounded the house we saw my father standing there in the yard.

In the doorway, the O'Malley girls stood.

In front of the step, Uncle Ronald stood.

"Me wife and me son!" my father shouted, throwing wide his arms.

My mother's hand went slowly up her opposite sleeve.

She spoke to me without opening her mouth and without looking at me and without moving.

"Go and stand behind your Uncle Ronald!" she said. "Now!"

"Oh, Nora," my father started. "Please forgive me. I'll change, I promise I will. All that is behind us now. Honest to God, Nora, everything will be different from now on, if you and the boy will only come back to me. I can't live without you. You and young Mickey. You won't regret it. You'll see. I have a new job and the money's just pourin' in...oh, Nora!"

He stopped to take a breath and then put his hand to his heart and started to sing a song I'd often heard him sing. He had a beautiful singing voice.

The violets were scenting the woods, Nora,
Displaying their charm to the bee,

When I first said I loved only you, Nora
And you said you loved only me.

The chestnut blooms gleamed through the glade, Nora,
A robin sang loud from a tree,
When I first said I loved only you, Nora
And you said you loved only me!

His voice echoed around the farm buildings.

"The violets and the bees are long gone, me bucko! And nobody's seen a chestnut tree in years. And the last news of the robins I heard was that they're gone south fer the winter!" my mother said in her best sarcastic voice. She sounded brave but she was shaking. She was terrified. Her eyes were closed and her eyelids were trembling.

"Oh, Nora!" my father moaned. "Don't be so hard and cruel. Don't you know I've learned the error of me ways? I swear to you in the name of everything that's holy. I will never touch a drop of intoxicatin' liquor again the rest of me born days! I need you, me darlin', me little puddin', me little berry. You're everything to me. I'm a wandering raftsman with no raft, no anchor, I'm lost...a sorrowful, pitiful man alone..."

He was dabbing the tears from his eyes into the shoulder of his red plaid jacket...

The golden-robed daffodils shone, Nora
And danced in the breeze on the lea
When I first said I loved only you, Nora
And you said you loved only me...

His voice was trembling and sounding full of love.

"You can drop the singin', Michael, we're not goin' back with you…" my mother said.

Her voice was even and sounded strong. You could tell he knew she meant it.

"Young Mickey has learned more with this family in a few days than he ever did in twelve years under your tender-loving care…" my mother said, looking over at me.

A wood warbler gave us his four high thin notes.

There was long silence.

Then my father's face and his body made a sudden change. His face darkened with anger and his body tensed.

"You and the boy," he said. "You're mine. You belong to me!"

"We belong to nobody! We belong to ourselves!" my mother said stout, raising her face and puffing out her chest.

"You won't come home with me?" my father said.

"No, we will not!" my mother answered, squaring her shoulders, her hand up her sleeve.

"You stole from me!" my father glared, his face like a storm.

"I took what was mine!" my mother shouted, her eyes squeezed shut.

"Well, then, I'll take what is mine, one way or the other!" my father growled and stepped toward my mother. His hands went to his waist, his fingers working the belt.

My mother didn't move. I knew she was clutching the knife handle hidden up her sleeve.

She stood her ground, trembling, her chin stuck out at him.

He stopped right over her. He hesitated. He seemed surprised by her bravery. Why wasn't she turning her face away, protecting herself with her arms? Ducking down? Backing up?

Then everything moved at once.

His hands on his belt.

Me running into him.

My hands on his belt.

His hands cuffing me away.

My face onto the hard clay of the yard.

The O'Malley girls' hands on my mother.

Uncle Ronald's hand on my father's fingers, squeezing.

Uncle Ronald saying, "You'll take nothing from here, Michael!"

My father sinking in pain to his knees. Uncle Ronald crushing his fingers.

"You'll leave us alone and you'll be on your way off this property and you'll not come back!" Uncle Ronald said, squeezing like a vice my father's cracking fingers.

Uncle Ronald letting go.

My father rising, backing out of the yard, screaming, holding his hand.

"You pack of twisters! You filthy squatters! You don't even pay your taxes! They send soldiers to squeeze a few tax dollars out of your measly hides!" His face was purple with rage.

"Yous' are a pack of thieves. And now you're stealin' from me. That woman, your little sister, and that boy, they're *my* property....Well, you'll pay for this, mister!" he snarled.

"Nobody, nobody steals from Mickey McGuire!"

Then he was turned and moving up the road, half running, leaning forward, holding his hand.

Beside my mother and at the feet of the O'Malley girls was their lost knife.

Everyone was frozen there, looking at the knife.

21

Heart of Lead

MY MOTHER WAS SITTING AT THE KITCHEN table, half crying, half laughing.

"You stood up to him!" the O'Malley girls were saying. "He has new respect for you now! Did you see him hesitate? He saw your strength. He'll think twice about comin' back!" the O'Malley girls said.

"Maybe we're free, Mickey, my boy. Maybe we're actually shook of him now!" my mother laughed and cried. Then she pounded the table.

"Mother of God," my mother cried, her face in her hands. "When I saw the difference between him and you!" She looked up at Uncle Ronald and the O'Malley girls. "The difference! I'd rather die than go back!"

Her face was flushed with bravery.

While Uncle Ronald put some of Willy Willis's ointment on my forehead where I scraped it on the hard clay of the yard, Even Steven came in the door to tell us he'd just been elected to another big-shot position, a special council to oversee the promises that everybody made. Father Foley and other big shots were also on the council.

We tried to explain to Steven what happened with my father but he was only half listening. His mind was on his new life as a big shot.

"What do you think he'll do?" Uncle Ronald asked my mother. "Will he go back to Ottawa?"

"Oh, I don't know," my
born and mean. He may try
you. To get even."

"Lance!" I yelled.

"He can't take Lance," Un
wouldn't let him. He'd never g
Lance would kick his head off b
harness him!"

"Lance *is* harnessed!" I yelle   ...ca: I
screamed and crashed out the door.

I rounded the house and looked up to the stable
with a sinking heart of lead.

Lance was gone!

22

Different-Sized Pieces of Something

STEVEN'S TEAM AND WAGON WERE READY. IN no time we were pounding down the road.

"He's a half hour ahead of us but he's not a horseman and he'll lose time at the gates and on the turns. Lance won't cooperate. He'll have trouble. And we can ask on the way. There's plenty of neighbors to help!"

Uncle Ronald was right. One of the gates was hanging open and the other one had a broken latch. Second Chance Lance wasn't cooperating.

At the sharp turn we saw my father's hat in the mud on the road.

About a mile outside of Low, Boner McCooey yelled that "a man in a hurry went by a while ago with your horse and rig! He was drinkin' out of a little bottle of whiskey, acting crazy!"

In Low, nobody saw anything. Everybody was strolling away from the station. They seemed a bit sad. The special train just left with the soldiers.

The fun was over.

In Brennan's Hill a woman with a pail at the pump in front of the store said the rig stopped for water a short while ago. She said the man was full of rage and the horse was frothing at the mouth and there seemed to be trouble with the rig or the harness or something.

About two miles down the road, just before Farrelton, we spotted them down a long curved turn.

Horse and rig and man didn't look quite right.

But they were moving at quite a clip.

My father was cutting Lance vicious with the whip. He snarled it up behind him and then over his head it coiled and writhed like a snapped steel cable. Then down with all the bulging of his shoulder and the hard thickness of his wrist onto the flanks of Second Chance Lance.

My father was an expert with a whip.

I knew then because of what Uncle Ronald had told me that my father had learned his lessons well. He learned the art of the whip from his own father. And now, he was teaching the belt and the whip to me. It wouldn't be long until I, too, knew it well and then passed the knowledge on to somebody else.

My unborn son, maybe.

And on and on.

But that never happened.

Because at that exact moment in my life, Second Chance Lance changed everything.

With his arm raised for another cut at Lance, my father hesitated. He heard something. So did we.

Then again. Clearer this time.

It was the sore-throat voice of the train. The train with razors in its throat.

The special train taking the soldiers back to Ottawa.

Down came the whip. Then, you could tell the way he all of a sudden moved that my father'd decided he'd beat the train to the level crossing ahead.

But then the next sad warning whistle was much closer. The voice of the train, again, something clawing at its throat. Angrier now.

Lance was doing a trot so fast his hooves were just a blur. Gobs of clay whizzed past my father's head.

Now my father for some reason changed his mind. Maybe it was the fierceness of the train whistle. And maybe the fact that he couldn't see the train at this point. You didn't see the train at this crossing until it was almost on top of you.

Whatever the reason, my father decided they weren't going to make the crossing in time. He lowered the whip and pulled the reins up short. Lance began to slow. They were coming up to the crossing.

"Whoa, whoa!" my father was roaring, although we couldn't hear him.

The breeching that Uncle Ronald had mended strained against Lance's rump.

My father, he was leaning back, pulling back the reins with all his weight, the bit in Lance's mouth ripping back, jerking back his head, dragging him up on his hind legs, screeching a high scream which we could almost hear, shaking his head and mane at the lead-colored sky, as if he was crying, "My mouth! my mouth!" and trying to get rid of the choking bit that pulled into his throat.

My father loosened the pressure on the reins and Lance was back on four legs and braced, front legs locked, back legs almost sitting, sliding, skidding to a stop on the greasy ancient clay.

The train came roaring through the cut like a monstrous angry rhino and headed across the tiny field to the crossing.

I see that picture now, one hundred years later, as plain as I see this old spotted bony hand of mine in front of this, my wrinkled old face.

♦

Lance stopping, trying to pull up.

But now Lance's whole harness is collapsing. The bellyband has loosened and everything's giving way. The britches aren't holding and the rig runs up onto the backs of Lance's legs.

Lance kicks and bolts across the track.

His move is so quick, so surprising that my father is thrown from the seat and loses the reins when he grabs for the side of the rig to hang on.

With his head down, digging with all his strength, Lance bursts across the track.

The engine clips the rear of the rig and bounces it, tipping it and spinning it into the ditch on Lance's side.

The blow sends my father up into the air and tumbling and rolling onto the track in front of the engine.

While the whistle howls and shrieks like a wounded animal, my father is gobbled up by the wheels and disappears under screaming steel and hissing steam and thundering iron.

♦

The end of the train was past by the time it got stopped. Lance was struggling to get to his feet, in the ditch, tangled in the twisted harness, kicking the rig into splinters.

The freight car doors were sliding open, soldiers leaning out to see what happened.

People ran up and down the train looking underneath. Soldiers and trainmen bent down walking along looking under. Then one trainman, a conductor, came out from between two cars. He had on his face a look of horror. He pointed behind himself.

"Here's something!" he called out. "There's something here!" he said without looking back.

Then he walked away.

We won't say much more than that about it.

Maybe just mention that after a lot of fuss, they got to put quite a few different sized pieces of something into a wooden box and cover it quick with army blankets.

23

Throw the Flower Hard

AFTER THE FUNERAL I TRIED THIS:

I looked in the mirror and held up my right hand. The boy who looked out of the mirror at me was holding up his *left* hand.

The answer to the riddle was easy. One of the O'Malley girls was left-handed, the other one right-handed!

It was at the graveyard that I saw it.

Father Foley gave us each a paper flower to drop in the hole after the ceremony.

There weren't very many people there. Uncle Ronald, the O'Malley girls, me, Even Steven, the two gravediggers standing well back, Father Foley and, for some reason, Sobbing McCooey, who, I guess, went every day to the graveyard, anyway.

When it came to my turn, I threw my flower hard into the hole instead of dropping it like the others did.

Father Foley gave me a look.

My mother and Sobbing McCooey were the only ones crying.

The O'Malley girls were the last to drop their flowers in.

They did it together.

Exactly the same.

Except for one thing.

One used her right hand, the other her left.

24

Clear as Crystal

SECOND CHANCE LANCE WAS RECOVERING quick from his injuries. He had cuts and bruises and scrapes that Willy Willis did his magic on.

It was the afternoon before Thanksgiving and Lance and Uncle Ronald and I waited on Even Steven's road—Uncle Ronald with his double-barrel shotgun ready. He stood in the slanting gold sun, clear as crystal.

The geese came sudden, blasting over the hill from Even Steven's field by the river.

Their discussion was deafening. The barking and honking and yodeling was the only sound in the world. There were three hundred of them in the formation.

Uncle Ronald picked one about three quarters back on the right leg of the V and fired.

The goose crumpled and fell. He picked another one from the left leg of the V and just a bit further back and pulled the other trigger. The second goose was tumbling before the first one hit the ground.

The space left by each goose was filled immediately by the ones behind.

"You never take the leaders," Uncle Ronald said. "Two reasons. The formation needs the leaders to get them out of here and further south where there's food for them in the winter months. Also, the smaller and younger ones nearer the rear are not as muscular, more tender."

"Do we need two geese?"

"Cecelia and Mr. Hickey are invited. And we're going to ask Even Steven."

"That's nice," I said.

"And while I'm sayin' grace before the dinner, I'm goin' to announce the engagement of Cecelia Hickey and Ronald O'Rourke!"

We went into the bush and brought out the geese.

As we tossed them into the rig, a snowflake flashed in the angling sun.

Lance was still wide-eyed and tense from the gunblasts.

"Snow!" Uncle Ronald said, surprise in his voice.

"Catch one of the first ones on your tongue," he said. "It's good luck!"

We moved around with our heads back and our tongues out, Lance watching us.

By the time we were halfway home, the snow was coming down thick and soft.

"We always know it's going to snow but when it does we're always surprised," Uncle Ronald said. "I wonder why that is?"

"It's because something is starting," I said, surprising myself with an idea that I didn't know I had.

Uncle Ronald was surprised, too. He looked at me, startled, his face full of wonder and love.

There!

Yes, and I remember like it was just now, the big cheer that went up at the Thanksgiving dinner table when Uncle Ronald made his announcement!

That was one hundred years ago.

I'm a very old man now. In fact, I'm Canada's oldest citizen.

And I'm back wetting the bed again. But it's not so bad now.

Just about everybody around here where I am wets the bed.

In fact, if you don't wet the bed around here, they think there's something wrong with you.

You won't be hearing from me any more, by the way. I'm going to die soon.

At least, I hope I am.

I don't particularly want to live any longer.

A hundred and twelve years is enough, don't you think?